KT-219-292

POPPY

Also by Mary Hooper

Historical fiction

At the Sign of the Sugared Plum
Petals in the Ashes
The Fever and the Flame
(a special omnibus edition of the two books above)
The Remarkable Life and Times of Eliza Rose
At the House of the Magician
By Royal Command
The Betrayal
Fallen Grace
Velvet
The Disgrace of Kitty Grey

Contemporary fiction

Megan
Megan 2
Megan 3
Holly
Amy
Chelsea and Astra: Two Sides of the Story
Zara

POPPY

MARY HOOPER

BLOOMSBURY

LONDON NEW DELHI NEW YORK SYDNEY

Bloomsbury Publishing, London, New Delhi, New York and Sydney

First published in Great Britain in May 2014 by Bloomsbury Publishing Plc
50 Bedford Square, London WC1B 3DP

Text copyright © Mary Hooper 2014

The moral right of the author has been asserted

Cover images:
Girl © Richard Jenkins
Poppies © Shutterstock
Wire © Benjamin Harte/Arcangel Images
Soldier © Stephen Mulcahey/Arcangel Images

All rights reserved
No part of this publication may be reproduced or transmitted by
any means, electronic, mechanical, photocopying or otherwise,
without the prior permission of the publisher

A CIP catalogue record for this book is available from the British Library

ISBN 978 1 4088 2762 8

Typeset by Hewer Text UK Ltd, Edinburgh
Printed and bound in Great Britain by CPI Group (UK) Ltd, Croydon CR0 4YY

1 3 5 7 9 10 8 6 4 2

www.bloomsbury.com
www.maryhooper.co.uk

For my Uncle Reg (Hewett), a conscientious objector in the Second World War

Chapter One

Poppy sat, bolt upright and uncomfortable, on one of the carved, wooden chairs in the blue drawing room of Airey House in the village of Mayfield. In front of her, looking equally out of place, sat Molly, the other parlourmaid. They were winding wool: Poppy had her arms outstretched with a long loop of wool around each hand, Molly was winding it into a ball, from right to left and back, catching Poppy's eye every now and again and giving her a *look*. Each time she did this, Poppy would have to glance away quickly or risk giggling.

Sitting around them in easy chairs were the ladies of the Mayfield Comforts Group, knitting balaclavas, gloves, socks and mufflers as fast as they could for the boys at the front. Since Poppy and Molly could only manage straight knitting – and because every garment apart from mufflers involved turning corners – Mrs Violet de Vere, matriarch of Airey House, had thought it best to ask her two parlourmaids to wind balls of wool from the long, loopy skeins. Being seated with servants was a little awkward for the comforts group ladies, for they couldn't speak as openly as they might have wished, but Mrs de Vere had realised that times were changing and she prided herself on being a modern employer. Also, by including Poppy and Molly, she had ensured that everyone was helping the war effort. That was important.

The ladies carried on clicking needles and Poppy and Molly wound on. Poppy thought of all the things she could be doing instead of sitting under the watchful eyes of the comforts group – and all the duties she would be scrambling to catch up with that afternoon, for an hour was a long interlude in a busy parlourmaid's day.

When their time in the drawing room was up, Mrs de Vere raised her eyebrows and gave Poppy a nod. This meant she and Molly were to disappear, change into their lace-trimmed afternoon aprons and return with pots of tea and a sponge cake. Once restored to their usual stations in life, the two girls served the ladies silently and deferentially and everyone was much more at ease.

As they poured and passed, the talk among the ladies was centred on the war, of course. Far from being 'over by Christmas' as everyone had predicted, it was escalating in many unforeseen ways, most recently with the bombardment and loss of life in Scarborough and the surrounding area. The ladies knew of several brave young men who had enlisted already, having been persuaded by Lord Kitchener that their country needed them. Mrs Trevin-Jones actually had a son fighting at the front, so her views on the war were treated with the utmost respect. Young Peter Trevin-Jones had not won any medals yet but the stories of his exploits suggested that it could only be a matter of time.

'My cousin's boy, Gerald, has taken a commission in the cavalry,' one lady interjected, having heard enough of Peter. 'He's been riding horses since he was two, so we expected no less.'

'Well, my grandson tried to enlist but, sadly, they wouldn't have him,' said another.

'Too young?'

'I don't believe there *is* such a thing!' came the reply. 'One is supposed to be over eighteen but apparently they don't even ask for identification. No, he had fallen arches so he wouldn't have been able to march. He was furious.'

'I expect his mother was pleased, though . . .' said another lady.

This was fiercely denied. 'His mother thought that fighting for his country would make a man of him. After all, what more noble ambition could there be for a boy?'

There were some murmurs of assent and a few sighs, too. Passing round porcelain teacups, Poppy wondered if her brother, Billy, might join up and, if so, whether war might make a man out of *him*.

Thinking about Billy always made Poppy rather cross, for he still hadn't managed to find himself a proper job.

He wouldn't consider going into service (he dismissed this as 'licking the boots of lords and ladies') and though he considered himself too good for factory work, he was not willing to go to evening classes to gain any paper qualifications for anything else. By the prudent pulling of strings, his uncle had managed to get him an interview for an office job, but Billy, being in a bad mood, had not interviewed well. He came back saying that the chief clerk was a stuffed shirt and he wouldn't take the job even if it was offered. Which it wasn't.

Poppy, however, had been working for the de Vere family ever since she left school at fourteen. She had won a scholarship to the local college, but with no father, and the college uniform and books costing more than her mother earned in a month of making cardboard boxes, she hadn't been able to take it up. At Airey House, the de Veres' home in Mayfield, just outside London, Poppy had started off in the kitchens and then, proving herself capable, had been elevated to a parlourmaid.

Slices of Victoria sponge were being eaten with silver forks when the door to the drawing room burst open and Mr Frederick de Vere, the youngest of the four de Vere children, came in looking cross. He was dressed in hunting gear – an old tweed jacket, plus fours and high leather boots – and looked unkempt in a rather dashing way. His appearance caused a little flurry of delight among the ladies of the circle, who sat up straighter and smiled indulgently at the sight of him. Poppy did *not* smile indulgently – she thought that *Master* Freddie (as

4

he was still called by most of the servants) was over-indulged by his mother and spoilt by his father. But then, that was the lot of all the de Vere children.

'Freddie!' cried Mrs de Vere, pleased that he'd arrived in time to be admired.

'Mother.' Freddie spoke in a leaden tone, then bent to kiss her powdery cheek. 'There's no one in the kitchen and I'm near starved to death.' He straightened up, caught Poppy's eye and gave her a wink.

Flip-flop. Poppy's heart skittered inside her and she turned away quickly, hoping she hadn't gone red. This had happened two or three times lately: he'd smiled at her for no apparent reason or pulled a quizzical face – and what he meant by it she couldn't imagine.

Freddie raked his hand through his hair, which was thick, fair, and fell into his eyes. 'Surely there should be someone who can fix a chap a bit of cold meat when he wants it.'

'Oh, of course, darling!' cried his mother. Her eyes – and those of the other ladies in the room – fell on the two maids. 'Well, Poppy?' she asked.

'Please, ma'am, there's no one there because it's Cook's afternoon off,' Poppy said.

Freddie pushed his hair back. 'I'm utterly starving . . .'

Poppy, wondering how difficult it would be for him to investigate the contents of the larder himself, looked towards Mrs de Vere for guidance.

'*If* you wouldn't mind fixing him something, Poppy,' said Mrs de Vere. She smiled round at the group. 'These boys, you know! Always ravenous.'

'Let him eat properly while he can,' Mrs Trevin-Jones said wisely. 'Peter has been existing on nothing but bully beef and hot water for *months*.'

Poppy picked up one of the trays and made for the door. As she did so, Freddie darted forward, pulled open the door and, making a mock bow, ushered her through.

'And no ox tongue, thank you, Poppy,' he said, his voice following her down the passageway. 'Just a knuckle of ham and maybe a few slices of roast beef.'

The door closed, but not before she heard one of the ladies asking Freddie what he intended to do for the war. The question was innocent enough, but most of the ladies present had been wondering why the two de Vere boys were still at home. They'd both attended good public schools and Jasper, the elder, had been to Oxford, but neither, as yet, had volunteered to serve his country, despite the fact that they were guaranteed commissions in a prestigious regiment. Both had, in fact, applied for exemption from military service on the grounds that they were needed at home to help manage the de Vere estate.

As Poppy arrived downstairs, Mrs Elkins, the de Veres' cook, was just hanging up her overcoat. She turned and surveyed Poppy, who was frowning deeply, then said, 'Oh dear, who's ruffled your feathers?'

'Master Freddie!' Poppy said.

'Not him again?'

'He's so . . . so impudent!'

'Oh, he's not that bad,' Mrs Elkins said, removing her felt hat. 'It's the way he's been raised. They ask and we provide.' She frowned slightly at Poppy. 'And it doesn't do to talk about any of the family like that, miss.'

'He seems to think we're all here to –'

'That's exactly what we *are* here for,' said Mrs Elkins. 'What else?' There was a jangle from the dining-room bell. 'Now, whoever's that? Would you go, dear?'

'That's him!' Poppy said. 'I bet that's him. He's gone into the dining room.'

'I'll make up a tray,' Mrs Elkins said, and she began to unpack the basket she'd come in with.

The bell rang again.

'Won't be a moment!' Cook trilled, though of course no one upstairs could hear her. The bell rang twice more and she sighed. 'Run up, Poppy, will you? Say I won't be a moment.'

Poppy groaned. 'Can't he just . . .'

Mrs Elkins turned and raised her eyebrows at her. Poppy went.

Entering the large dining room, which was empty except for Freddie standing by the bell pull, Poppy bobbed a curtsey. If only he wasn't quite so good-looking, she thought. If only his hair wasn't so floppy or his eyes such a deep brown . . .

'Yes, sir?'

'I just wanted you to know that I was in here, in the dining room.'

Poppy hesitated, fighting against an inner desire to say that she wasn't entirely daft. She managed another curtsey – the slightest curtsey possible. 'Yes, thank you, Master Freddie.'

He smiled. 'You know, just *Freddie* will do.'

'Oh. Well.' Surprised and rather alarmed, Poppy took a step towards the door. 'Cook is back now, and if you'll allow me to go down again then we'll bring you up a tray.'

She would get Molly to do it, she thought, or Mrs Elkins. What with the wink, and then being told she could call him Freddie, she felt all of a dither. Besides, it really wasn't proper for him to tease her in this way. It was almost as if he was . . . But no, *that* was ridiculous.

Chapter Two

Stanley and Lily Pearson had not intended to call her after a red field flower. Wanting to give their children plain names, they had already decided that if the coming baby was a girl, she would be called Ann. When she arrived after several hours' labour, however, red in the face and screaming, with a few wispy, gingery curls, the midwife said, 'Look at this one – red as a poppy!' and the name had stuck. Her earlier carroty hair had softened over the years to a gentle pink-blond, but Poppy still had the complexion of a redhead, with fine, almost translucent skin and green eyes. She was born just a year before Billy, and then two further girls had come into the family, Jane and Mary, then another boy, who died after a few weeks.

There were four de Vere children also. Mrs de Vere liked things orderly and considered it a fine achievement to have produced two children of each sex: the girls first, then the boys, with an almost exact two-year gap between each of them. The girls, Bonita and Susannah de Vere – long-haired and, at that time, rather insipid – had come out in London society at sixteen, had had a photographic portrait in *Country Life* and attended Queen Charlotte's Ball. Here they and other pretty, well-bred girls had sashayed about in white gowns, hoping to bump into eligible young men and be proposed to. Just as tradition dictated, they had curtseyed to a huge white birthday cake, danced every dance, fallen in love and, quite soon after, been married. Bonita's husband was titled, but Susannah's was rich, and each girl considered herself the luckier. They had done very little with their days until war had been declared, but now Bonita was working as a recruiter, undertaking clerical work at her local town hall for the boys who wanted to join up. Susannah, her husband's farm having lost a dozen workers to the war, had helped form a group of young women into the beginnings of the Women's Land Army to ensure there were enough workers to bring in the harvest. Both girls found work outside the home surprisingly invigorating and were no longer insipid.

All the de Veres were back at Airey House for Christmas 1914, though Mrs de Vere had deliberately played down the festive table and it was not, as in previous years, groaning under the weight of stuffed goose and capon, fruit trifles and crème caramels. Rationing had not yet been introduced, but Poppy and everyone else knew that to pile a dining table with luxury foods was not appropriate during wartime. Thus the Christmas tree in the hall (which came from the estate) was simply hung with homemade crêpe-paper flowers and some little wooden robins which Freddie had carved. Instead of rich plum puddings for the festive period, Mrs Elkins had made cakes from leftover bread and soups which didn't taste of very much. Everyone ate up without fuss, feeling that by doing so they were somehow aiding the war effort.

On the morning of 26th December, the de Veres' servants were summoned into the blue drawing room to receive their Christmas boxes and take a small glass of sherry with the family. The gifts were always the same: male servants received a half bottle of whisky, female staff a pair of leather gloves. There were fewer staff this year as Mrs Reid the housekeeper had gone to be a bus conductor, several young valets had joined the army and two of the female house servants had gone to work in a munitions factory. The thought of life outside the de Vere household, of becoming independent whilst helping the fight in some small way, was becoming more and more attractive to all the servants, especially as it now seemed that the war was not going to end anytime soon.

Mrs de Vere spoke about the difficulties and shortages the family had faced in the past months and, handing the staff their gifts, thanked them for their loyalty and said that, whether peace or war prevailed, the family trusted they could rely on them in the coming year.

The servants made murmurs of assent, finished their sherry and turned to file out, at which point Jasper de Vere got to his feet and raised his hand to halt them. 'One moment, if you please.'

Everyone stopped.

He gestured around the room. 'There's something I wish to say not only to my parents and family, but to you all . . .'

Poppy knew what was coming before he said it, merely from the proud tone he used.

'I have today heard from the War Office that they have been good enough to offer me a commission in the Royal Engineers. Mother, Father, I am to serve my country as a second lieutenant in the British Army.'

'Oh!' Mrs de Vere flushed pink. 'Oh, my darling!'

Mr de Vere moved to slap his son on the shoulder. 'Jolly good show,' he said. 'I'd go myself if they'd have me!'

The servants began clapping. Poppy noticed that the only one who didn't look frightfully pleased about it all was Freddie. This was not, she quickly realised, because he was going to miss his brother, but because it made him, still at home carving robins when his country was crying out for recruits, look rather pathetic. However, he would have an even better excuse for not going to war now, as the only son left to help his father on the estate.

Poppy, staring at him and thinking about his life, was startled when Freddie turned and looked directly at her. There was a certain look on his face and afterwards she tried to put a name to what sort of a look it had been: vulnerable, enquiring . . . and somehow *interested*. She couldn't exactly explain *how* he'd looked, but it was not the usual sort of look between a de Vere and a parlour-maid. Her cheeks went pink and, looking away, she pretended to study her new gloves. How had that happened, she wondered. How had he gone from being merely the younger de Vere boy to someone who could quicken her heart?

The applause from the servants died down and, before they could move off again, Mr de Vere rose to his feet. 'This seems an opportune time to pass on an item of news about the war,' he said. 'In the *Telegraph* this morning there was a report of a Christmas truce on the front line.'

'Oh, how marvellous!' cried Mrs de Vere.

'Apparently,' continued her husband, 'yesterday – Christmas morning – our Tommies and the German soldiers called greetings to each other, then ventured out of their trenches into no-man's-land to exchange food and souvenirs. It's said that they played games of foot-ball, England against Germany – bartered cigarettes and shook hands for a happy new year.'

'There!' said Freddie. 'Perhaps it's true what some people are saying: that the war isn't so serious and soon everyone will be home again.'

'I fear it *is* serious,' said his brother, a trace of reproof in his tone. 'Hundreds have already been killed at Marne.'

'Yes, of course, dear,' said Mrs de Vere, as if sensing a little tension between her two boys. 'I'm very much afraid that they have.'

'At any rate, the generals didn't approve of the cease-fire,' said Jasper. 'Any fraternisation between Tommy and Fritz is frowned upon.'

'Quite,' said Mr de Vere, who'd had several glasses of port wine. 'They think that if the lads get too friendly they won't be so keen to knock the blasted bejesus out of each other!'

At this Mrs de Vere raised her eyebrows at her husband. Everyone fell silent and the servants finally left the room.

A group of guests had been invited for afternoon tea on New Year's Day. There had been much discussion between Cook and Mrs de Vere on what, exactly, this tea should consist of. The latter wanted to strike the right note: mindful of the war, but not too frugal with the iced fancies in case she was deemed as lacking in hospitality.

At four o'clock, going into the drawing room bearing the best silver teapot, Poppy was all-over anxious to see one particular person, for a Miss Philippa Cardew and her family were amongst the guests. This Miss Cardew – so rumours below stairs had it – was in line to marry Master Freddie. ('Money marrying money,' Mrs Elkins told Poppy. 'No love involved – you mark my words – just land and country houses.')

Setting down the tea tray on the polished table, Poppy took in the visitors at a glance and knew immediately which one was Miss Cardew, for she was the only female of the right age and, besides, was terribly attractive and stylish, with bobbed hair which fell straight and shiny to her jaw in the new fashion. She was wearing a bias-cut dress in bright emerald silk with a full pink rose pinned at the neckline, and had matching pink satin boots with a row of buttons running up the sides.

Poppy was somewhat taken aback. Just an alliance of land and country houses, Mrs Elkins had said, and Poppy had somehow imagined Miss Cardew as a solid, frumpy country girl, with bird's-nest hair and thick knitted stockings. She hadn't prepared herself for the possibility of beauty.

The likelihood of Freddie and Miss Cardew becoming engaged was discussed over the servants' tea break, but Poppy, despite being full of thoughts on the matter, did not volunteer any opinion either way.

At five o'clock she was delighted to have her mood lifted when Cook remembered that a letter for her had been delivered by second post. It was from Miss Luttrell, her old English teacher.

The Pantiles,
Mayfield, Herts

31ˢᵗ December 1914

My dear Poppy,
Thank you for your Christmas card. I was pleased to hear of your doings and know that you and your family

are all well. I still occasionally see your mother when I am popping in and out of the village shops and we always exchange the latest news. News about you, I mean!

Poppy, as you know, I was very disappointed that you could not go on to take a higher qualification at college, but I have recently heard of an exciting and fulfilling opportunity that I think would be perfect for you – and would also offer training of practical use after the war. I know you are content at the de Veres', but I long to see you doing something which would use your intelligence and really stretch you. I am also of the opinion that as many of us as possible should be helping the war effort. There! Have I aroused your curiosity?

I know you have very little spare time but wondered if you would be able to meet me on your next day off. I am about to leave Mayfield for some weeks to stay with my sister in Kensington, and thought that a meal in London would be a treat for both of us. There is a Lyons Corner House in the Strand, opposite Charing Cross station – perhaps you could meet me there?

If you are interested in hearing what I have to say to you, please do drop me a line with a suggested date. In the meantime, allow me to wish you the compliments of the season. Yours truly,

Enid Luttrell

'Ooh, you've got a letter!' Molly said, trying to look over her shoulder. 'Who's it from? Is it a *love* letter?'

'No, of course not! It's actually from my old English teacher,' Poppy explained. 'She's retired now, but we still keep in touch – she's a dear old stick.'

'But what does she want?'

Poppy smiled. 'To stand me dinner! Lyons Corner House in the Strand.'

Molly's eyes widened. 'Grand!'

'She's probably going to give me a lecture on women's suffrage.' On Molly looking at her blankly, she added, 'You know, women getting the vote. She was very keen on that before the war started.'

'Oh well,' said Molly. 'It'll be worth it for the lunch!'

Poppy smiled and nodded, then folded the letter and her new gloves and tucked them both carefully into her apron pocket. She wouldn't think about Miss Cardew and she wouldn't think of Freddie. She would think of Miss Luttrell's letter and the possibility of an exciting and fulfilling opportunity . . .

Chapter Three

It was well into January when Poppy could get time off to meet Miss Luttrell in London. She went from the local station by steam train to Euston, and from there was only a little terrified to find herself travelling on the Underground to Trafalgar Square.

The Strand was full of khaki-clad soldiers and thrillingly busy. There were many indications that there was a war on: advertisements on billboards urged *Send a jar of Bovril to your Tommy at the front* or emphasised that *Bread gives us the strength to win the fight*, and hoardings and omnibuses alike bore a variety of posters persuading all able-bodied men to enlist in the army and serve their country. Poppy sighed when she saw these, almost wishing that she had someone marching off to fight the good fight; someone to worry about, to knit a scarf for and send parcels to. A sweetheart would be best, but – failing that – even a brother would do.

For the first time, Poppy saw men wearing the blue cotton suits which signified that they were soldiers on day release from the hospitals. Some of these men were missing a limb or limping badly. One who passed her had only one eye and a ghastly, livid scar which ran from his temple, across his cheek and right down his neck, so that Poppy had to brace herself not to turn away from him in horror. People greeted these men warmly, clapping them on the shoulder and shaking their hands, for they were war heroes and had the wounds to prove it.

Miss Luttrell had not yet arrived at the Corner House, so Poppy, enjoying being addressed as 'madam' and the novelty of being deferred to, asked the waitress for a window table for two. From here she could look on to the vast station concourse at Charing Cross and watch the minor dramas being enacted outside: people meeting and kissing, parting and crying, soldiers weighed down with mighty loads of equipment, businessmen in top hats or bowlers, children with nursemaids, and a lady at the wheel of a shiny open car that was bellowing out yards of smoke (her chauffeur must have gone into the army, Poppy decided). One surprising thing was that many well-to-do ladies appeared to be unchaperoned. She had read features in the family's discarded newspapers about this. It seemed that ladies whose husbands were at war felt that they no longer needed a man to escort them to film matinees or a maid to scurry behind them carrying their parcels – they could manage perfectly well by themselves. Indeed, wealthy lady shoppers whose chauffeurs had joined the army were driving themselves to eat in restaurants with their female companions. They were wearing bloomers, too: on pedal cycles, to attend exercise classes – or just because they wanted to.

When Miss Luttrell advanced across the restaurant floor – wearing a dark tweed suit, brown woolly hat and eager expression – Poppy's first thought was that she hadn't changed a bit in all the time that she'd known her. Did elderly ladies, she wondered, reach a certain standard of oldness and then stay the same? Unsure of how to greet her, Poppy stood at her approach just as she'd done when Miss Luttrell had come into the school room, but was waved at to sit down again.

'My dear child, we don't stand on ceremony these days,' said Miss Luttrell, pecking Poppy on the cheek.

Poppy sat down. 'It's really very nice to see you,' she said, smiling and a little shy at the strangeness of the occasion. 'It's been about a year, I think.'

'How time flies!' Miss Luttrell reached for the printed tariff and ran a finger down the choices. 'I expect you're hungry, dear. Shall we order straight away?'

Poppy nodded, starving because she'd been too excited at the thought of the outing to eat breakfast that morning.

Miss Luttrell held the tariff at arm's length and got the words into focus. 'The steak and tomato pie is always good here, or the braised tongue is a very substantial meal. They both come with mashed potato and vegetable marrow.'

The idea of ox tongue didn't appeal to Poppy and she and Miss Luttrell both decided to order a pie. When the waitress left them, they stared outside for a moment, where an army truck filled with soldiers had pulled up. A small crowd gathered to watch them and cheer as they fell into ranks and marched in formation under the vast arch of the station.

'Another legion of our brave boys marching to death or glory!' Miss Luttrell said, and then, rather embarrassingly, stood up and applauded them (though no one outside the shop could have heard her) so that Poppy felt she had to stand and clap too.

When the soldiers had all disappeared, Miss Luttrell sat down again. 'Now, do tell me what you're doing.'

Poppy started on a list of her regular duties at the de Vere house, but was stopped almost immediately.

'I meant, what are you doing for the *war*?' Miss Luttrell asked.

Poppy thought. 'On my own, I suppose not very much, but Cook makes what she calls economy puddings and the household is saving on fuel – we're never allowed a fire in our bedrooms.'

'I expect the family still have fires in *their* rooms, though,' said Miss Luttrell drily. She knew the de Vere family: they gave an annual allowance to the local school in Mayfield where she used to teach, and she and Mrs de Vere occasionally found themselves serving on the same charity board.

Poppy didn't reply to this little barbed comment, for the family did indeed still have fires in their rooms. 'Mrs de Vere has a knitting circle making comforts for the men at the front,' she suddenly remembered. 'I go to that once a week.'

'Ah, *comforts*,' Miss Luttrell said rather disparagingly. 'I believe the men are weighed down by so-called *comforts*. I've heard that they have so many they clean their rifles with them.' She adjusted her hat. 'But has Mrs de Vere encouraged her sons to go and fight for the cause?'

Poppy nodded. 'Jasper de Vere has enlisted. He's just started his training with the Royal Engineers.'

'Not before time! And the other boy?'

Poppy was torn. She wanted to denounce Freddie as a war refuser, but it seemed rather disloyal to the de Vere family, who paid her wages and, on the whole, were good to her. And besides, there were those rather perplexing looks Freddie had been giving her lately.

'At the moment he's working on the estate,' she said lamely.

Miss Luttrell raised her eyebrows. 'While other boys of his age are deep in mud and dodging bullets in the trenches!'

Poppy hesitated. 'I know it doesn't sound right –'

'He's a coward! Someone should present him with a white feather. I'd do it myself if I wasn't living in London.'

Poppy's eyes widened. She knew that for a man to be presented with a white feather was the greatest shame – so much so that the government had issued exemption certificates and badges to be given to men in certain trades to show if anyone asked them why they weren't in uniform.

'Perhaps you could give him one,' said Miss Luttrell briskly. 'After all, why shouldn't he fight? The privileged rich have even more reason than the rest of us to make sure this country isn't overrun by Fritz.'

'I couldn't . . .'

'My dear, it's your duty. Haven't you seen the posters?'

'The recruitment posters?' Poppy nodded.

'Especially the one showing women standing at an open window watching their nearest and dearest marching off to fight.' Miss Luttrell raised her voice and cried, '*Women of Britain say – "GO!"* '

Several people in the restaurant turned to look at her.

'No, I haven't seen that one yet,' Poppy said hastily.

'No one need know the feather has come from you,' Miss Luttrell resumed. 'You could leave it at his place at the dinner table perhaps. Or even put it in the post.'

'But I couldn't do that to F– I mean, Mr de Vere.' Poppy was quiet for a moment, then she said with a sigh, 'My brother's the same, though, Miss Luttrell. He hasn't even got the excuse of having an estate to look after.'

'Then he must also have a white feather!' When Poppy didn't reply to this, she added, 'Our country needs every one of our boys to be ready to fight. We women should be hardening our hearts and playing our part in getting them there.' She looked searchingly at Poppy. 'As for you, my dear, you have a *brain*. You could be playing a far more useful part in the war instead of plumping madam's cushions and making sure her card table is dusted.'

'I suppose so,' Poppy said. 'Some of the staff at the house have already moved on. Our housekeeper has gone to be a bus conductor, Cook's girl is working as a clerk in an office and some of the others have gone to take the men's places in factories.'

'As a matter of fact I wasn't thinking of factory work for you.' Miss Luttrell paused, then said earnestly, 'I was going to suggest that you become a nurse, a member of the army's Voluntary Aid Detachment.'

'Oh!' Poppy said, surprised. She had never considered nursing, much less considered it in wartime. She'd seen pictures on the newsreels of field hospitals near the front line, with rows of camp beds and nurses, as silent and compassionate as angels, flitting up and down the rows tending to their patients. Her only thought on seeing them had been that they must be awfully decent girls.

Their meal arrived and during the first few mouthfuls neither of them spoke, for Poppy was thinking about things, wondering if she could . . . if she should . . .

It was Miss Luttrell who resumed the conversation. 'I saw how well you nursed your mother when she was so poorly after her last child.'

Poppy nodded, remembering the dark times just after Barney had been born. Her mother had been very seriously ill then – hysterical and sweating with child-bed fever – and Poppy had nursed her day and night. Tragically, little Barney, always weak, had died when he was a few weeks old. With her father not long dead and her two sisters still very young, it had been a terrible period for her family. She'd coped – just about – but she'd been caring for a close relative then, she thought; someone she loved, not some anonymous stranger. On the other hand, perhaps it would be easier to nurse someone she wasn't emotionally attached to – and it would be rather wonderful to become one of those nurses with a starched white uniform bearing a red cross, so highly thought of, so revered.

'At present I'm doing some Red Cross work,' Miss Luttrell said. In response to Poppy's look of surprise she added, 'Oh, I don't mean actual nursing. I haven't the energy for that – it's terrifically hard work. What I do is serve in army canteens, handing out cigarettes and cocoa to our chaps, and I roll bandages and cut gauze into wads for the dressing of wounds.'

She stopped speaking for a moment and they both looked out of the window at a man, with a bandage which went round his head and completely covered both eyes, walking with uncertain steps. Another man was holding his arm and guiding him between obstacles. Poppy silently prayed that Miss Luttrell wouldn't stand up and applaud again and, luckily, she was too involved in saying her piece to do so.

'You're just the sort of girl they're looking for to be a VAD,' Miss Luttrell went on. 'Young, enterprising, healthy, intelligent. You could make a real difference.'

Poppy's brow furrowed, trying to see herself in that role. 'But I've never thought about *nursing*. I don't know if I . . .'

'Volunteers get two or three months' training before they're allowed on a ward,' Miss Luttrell said, 'and they always work under a sister's guidance.'

'Yes, but you just called them *volunteers*,' Poppy said. 'So they don't get paid.'

'They get their board and lodging, just as you do at the de Veres'. You'd live in a hostel with other trainee nurses.'

'But I send half my wages home to Mother,' Poppy said. 'I wouldn't be able to do that if I were a nurse, would I? She really needs what I send.'

'No, you wouldn't have wages as such.' She smiled. 'But, my dear, I have a proposition for you.'

Poppy, intrigued, waited while Miss Luttrell finished her pie and gathered her thoughts.

'I've been left a small annuity by an ancient relative,' she said eventually. 'I don't need it all, and I'd like to share it with you – if you'd let me.'

Poppy's jaw dropped. 'But I couldn't possibly!' she said automatically.

Miss Luttrell went on as if she hadn't heard, 'The pity of it is, if I'd been left the money a few years ago I could have helped pay for your college education.'

'That really is too kind,' Poppy protested.

'If you wanted to join as a VAD I'd be able to provide you with an allowance – one that would be about the same as the wages you earn now,' Miss Luttrell continued.

'That's terribly generous, but –'

'I think you might find that, when the war is over, you want to stay in nursing and obtain some proper qualifications. It's a fine career for a woman. Maybe you could even study to be a doctor. I think you'd be capable of it.'

'Never!' Poppy exclaimed. It was true, she *was* becoming a little bored at the de Vere house, but she hadn't given much thought to what she could do instead of being a parlourmaid. Could she really become a nurse?

'I don't see why not!' said Miss Luttrell.

An amount of time elapsed before Poppy, chewing her lip, asked, 'Can I let you know? It's most awfully good of you, but I must think about it.'

'My dear, of course you must give it proper consideration!' Miss Luttrell pushed her empty plate away and rummaged in her handbag. 'In the meantime, do please take these two white feathers and give them out as you see fit. Remember: *every* young man should enlist and fight for his country. And you know, in your heart, who deserves to be given one . . .'

Chapter Four

The feathers were small and soft and curled. Poppy put them in her coat pocket but somehow contrived to lose one of them between Euston and Mayfield stations. She pretended to be cross with herself, but was actually rather relieved. She'd already decided that, before presenting her brother with such a thing, she ought to give him a chance and would have a good and sober talk with him. Surely if she explained how important playing his part was, if she told him how desperately regular Tommies were needed, if she spoke to him seriously, he would agree that he must join the army.

That left one feather for Freddie de Vere.

But should she really give it to him – and exactly how should she do it? She'd seen pictures in the newspapers of resolute women standing outside public houses, feathers in hand, ready to accost any able-bodied man who wasn't in uniform. She knew she'd never have the nerve to just present him with it – and anyway, this would surely mean instant dismissal from the de Veres. Leaving the feather in Freddie's room was out of the question, too – with the diminishing number of staff in the house only a few had access to it so she was bound to be suspected.

As for training as a nurse – well! It was a fine and noble calling, but did *she* wish to be fine and noble? What would her mother have to say about it? Would she enjoy living in a hostel in some strange city with a crowd of girls she didn't know? Posh girls, too, she'd heard.

Lying in bed that night, Poppy went over her options. She'd seen and admired the VAD nurses, but if she became one, what sights might she have to see? What gruesome tasks would she have to undertake? She was not especially squeamish, but she knew that many unfortunate men came back from the war with such horrendous injuries that not even their own mothers could face looking at them. Living with the de Veres might be tedious some-times, but at least it was clean, safe and uncomplicated.

Ten indecision-filled days had passed after her meeting with Miss Luttrell when Poppy received the following letter.

The Pantiles,
Mayfield, Herts

12th February 1915

My dear Poppy,
I wonder if you have thought any more about my offer? Not wishing to rush you or influence you too much, but I

have this week spoken to one of the nursing sisters at Devonshire House in London, where they recruit VADs. She told me they are sending so many girls to France that they are in urgent need of more volunteers for the new military hospitals that have been set up here at home. Now would be an ideal time to enlist!

I went to Dover last week with a dozen nurses to meet a shipful of injured lads coming home, and was able to see at first-hand how much comfort they derived from being looked after by girls with cheery smiles and solicitous manners. Some of these lads hadn't seen an English girl for months, and all seemed most grateful for the care and attention they received, even down to trying to make light of their injuries and apologising for the inconvenience when they needed moving from stretcher to bed and so on. They seemed to have kept their sense of humour, too: 'If you think I look bad, you should have seen the chap who whopped me!' I heard more than once.

But even if you decide against VAD work, let me know how things are going at the de Veres. I am anxious to hear if the white feathers had any effect on their recipients? With kindest regards,

Enid Luttrell

This letter didn't stir Poppy into making a decision about nursing, but she decided she would send Freddie the remaining white feather, feeling that it would keep

Miss Luttrell at bay a while longer. It was for his own good, she thought, for the newspapers were full of stories about young men being jostled and shouted at in the street because they weren't in uniform. Not signing up to fight for their country was, in some people's eyes, tantamount to helping the enemy. In Poppy's heart of hearts, however, and even though Miss Luttrell had almost convinced her that it was a woman's sacred duty to persuade the men in her life to fight, she wasn't altogether happy about doing such a thing.

Knowing that she really didn't have the nerve to give Freddie the feather in person, Poppy went to the village post office, bought a ready-stamped envelope and then, writing Freddie's name and address in a disguised hand, enclosed the feather within a piece of folded paper. It would arrive with the Mayfield postmark on it, but the village contained nearly three hundred people and it could have come from any one of them.

The letter arrived – much earlier than Poppy had anticipated – at the de Vere household the next morning. On this particular day, as luck would have it, the de Veres had several guests staying for a few days of shooting. Miss Philippa Cardew and her brother, Toby, were among them.

At breakfast-time Poppy took a large serving bowl of porridge into the dining room. Seeing the letter beside Freddie's plate and only then fully realising the impact it was going to have, she was filled with trepidation. She could scarcely believe she'd done such a thing.

As Poppy moved around the table serving everyone, her hands began shaking. She even considered dropping the cream jug on the letter to try to get it out of the room, but abandoned that idea because breaking it would make her look foolish.

All the talk at table was of the war and of the first Zeppelin raids. These strange, surreal-looking airships had dropped high-explosive bombs in Norfolk in January and it was greatly feared that if the London docks were targeted it would mean considerable damage to the British fleet.

The war talk didn't prevent the de Veres and their company enjoying a hearty breakfast. When Mr de Vere asked for sausages as well as black pudding, Poppy was thankful to leave the room to get them, hoping that, if she took her time, the letter opening might happen in her absence.

When she returned, however, Freddie was just pulling up the flap of the envelope.

'How curious! Someone has sent me a blank piece of paper,' he said. He pulled out the folded sheet and the white feather slowly, gracefully fluttered down on to the table.

Poppy turned away and heard him draw in his breath sharply.

There was a moment's horrified silence and then Philippa Cardew gave a nervous laugh. 'Oh, I say, Freddie! You've been caught by the Order of the White Feather.'

Poppy moved to the sideboard and began to cut more bread. She wished – oh, how she wished – she hadn't done it!

'Well, they shouldn't have sent it . . . It's not right,' said Freddie, his face as pale as the porcelain breakfast plates. 'I've got – at least, I'm getting – a reserved occupation card.'

'It's a damned bad show. Not necessary at all,' blustered Mr de Vere.

'These women, sending out feathers willy-nilly, eh?' said Toby Cardew. 'You don't see *them* fighting in the trenches.'

'There *are* women just behind the front line,' his sister said immediately. 'They put their lives at risk every day, bringing in and tending the wounded.'

Her brother shrugged uncomfortably. 'Well, yes . . .'

'Haven't you got an exemption badge to wear, old chap?' one of the other young men in the party asked.

'No, not as yet,' Freddie admitted, his face now flushed rather than pale. 'I, er, think it's on its way.'

'The feather must have been sent from someone in the village,' Mrs de Vere said indignantly, studying the envelope. 'Someone who obviously doesn't know how important Freddie's work is here, helping with the estate.'

'I suppose a woman whose own son has gone to fight might –' Mr de Vere began, to be stopped by a look from his wife.

'It's a pretty bad show. I'm no coward,' said Freddie. But his voice quavered as he spoke and Poppy discovered

33

that not only did she desperately wish she hadn't humili-
ated him, but she also wanted to comfort him and
smooth away the little frown lines that had appeared on
his forehead. 'If you'll excuse me . . .' Pushing back his
chair from the table so abruptly that it screeched on the
wooden floor, he went out, not reappearing again in the
breakfast room until a good half hour had passed.

Poppy avoided Freddie whenever she could after that.
But then, two days later, it was two o'clock in the morning, and Poppy couldn't sleep. Beside her, Molly was
snoring gently, though it wasn't her who was keeping
Poppy awake, but the thought of the dishonour she'd
brought down on Freddie in front of his friends and
family. They had all tried to make light of the feather's
delivery, but it was not a light matter and it had caused
Freddie to become so uncomfortable and embarrassed
that the party had broken up and the visitors departed
shortly before lunch. The other thing that was keeping
Poppy from sleeping was her reaction to seeing Freddie
so disconcerted – she'd wanted to wind her arms around
his neck, place her cool cheek against his burning one
and make him feel better. This feeling was surely ridiculous, she told herself, and could only lead to an unhappy
ending. Going silly over a de Vere boy – whatever was
she thinking of?

She turned this way and that in the bed, accidentally
kicking Molly more than once, but was unable to unravel

her feelings and put Freddie out of her mind. As she lay there counting her companion's snores, she heard a strange humming noise: a droning, as if a large bumble-bee had been caught behind the window blind. For a moment, she thought it *was* a bee, and strained to see across the room in the darkness. The humming became louder, though, and more puzzling, and in the end she made herself get out of bed to investigate.

She lifted a corner of the blind and peered down on to the gravelled drive, thinking that it must be a car or some sort of machinery. There was nothing to be seen, however. Deciding that it was something in the house that was making the noise, she was about to go back to bed when the moon came out and suddenly, startlingly, she saw that there was a great silver shape gliding across the sky.

'A Zeppelin!' she said. As Molly stirred in the bed, Poppy called in an excited whisper, 'Look at this, Molly. Come quickly!'

She pressed her face against the cold pane, staring up at the great oval ship sailing high, shimmering in the moonlight. She hadn't seen one in real life before, and it looked so strange and unearthly sliding in and out of the clouds.

'Come and look at the Zeppelin!' she urged Molly again.

But Molly only grunted and wriggled further under the blankets.

'I'm going outside to see it properly,' said Poppy. Not wanting to waste time looking for her dressing gown and slippers, she rushed down the back stairs.

She was slightly surprised that half the household wasn't out there marvelling at the sight in the sky, but there was no one on the drive. The great front lawn was empty except for the group of Romanesque statues which stood around the lake.

Oblivious to the cold, Poppy slipped across the lawn like a wraith, her bare feet leaving imprints in the wet grass. It was a different and magical world at night: the tips of the trees glittery with rime, the stars twinkling dots of silver and the moonlight sparkling on the water. The Zeppelin was very high and seemed to be London bound. Did it carry bombs, Poppy wondered, or was it on a spying mission? She prayed that it didn't carry ammunition and that London would be safe tonight.

'It's hard to believe that something so perfectly formed can cause such destruction,' a voice behind her said.

Poppy, startled into thinking that one of the statues had spoken, started with fright.

'I don't think that one means us any harm tonight, though,' the voice went on. Poppy saw with some relief that what she'd thought was one of the cloaked statues was, in fact, Freddie de Vere with an eiderdown thrown about his shoulders.

'No, nor do I,' she breathed.

He moved to stand beside her. 'I think it's just on a reconnaissance mission.'

Poppy, feeling some explanation of her presence in the garden at this hour was called for, spoke nervously. 'I couldn't sleep and then I heard this noise and I had to . . .'

'Quite, quite,' said Freddie, and he gazed once more at the great silver ship. 'I was sleepless, too.'

There was a long moment of silence between them. He was standing on her right, just an inch away, and Poppy knew she only had to stretch out her fingers and they would touch his. The desire to actually do this suddenly became so strong that she made herself take a step away from him.

'If you'll excuse me, sir,' she said, 'I ought to be going in.'

'Oh, don't leave on my account,' Freddie said, and he turned to her and smiled a smile which was going to cause her several sleepless nights. 'And, please – less of the *sir*. Freddie will do nicely.'

'I . . . I couldn't.'

'Of course you could.' He glanced at her again. 'How long have you been working for my family, Poppy?'

'Four years,' Poppy said.

'Four years! But for most of that time I was away at school, of course.'

Poppy stood, herself as silent and still as a statue.

'The funny thing is, I feel that I only really saw you – noticed you – when I finished school and came back here at the end of November.'

Half dizzy with a combination of amazement and lack of sleep, Poppy didn't speak.

'And then, when I *did* notice you . . .'

His eyes held hers and Poppy, unable to resist any

longer, reached to clasp his hand at the same moment he did. The instant their fingers touched, however, she became frightened of what was happening. Suddenly realising that her nightdress was thin and gauzy, she turned away from him and fled back across the dew-soaked lawn without another word.

When she reached her bedroom, quite out of breath, she looked out of the window and saw Freddie was still out there, staring into the clouds which had enveloped the airship.

Too stirred up to sleep, she was awake for the rest of the night. She'd nearly taken his hand! How brazen he must think her. But then, *he* had started it. She didn't have much experience with boys, but could tell from the way he'd spoken and the way he'd looked at her that . . . Well, she didn't know exactly *what* she knew, she just knew some-thing was happening. Something between the two of them . . .

The next morning, with Jasper de Vere away doing his military training and just three members of the family in the dining room, Poppy felt a little awkward carrying in the breakfast tray. She wondered if Freddie was embarrassed about last night and regretted having spoken to her. He just glanced up at her, however, gave a slight nod and then resumed his conversation with his mother and father.

'Yes, it was the strangest sight to see,' he said, as Poppy

placed a jug of cream by his plate. 'Rather wonderful and other-worldly.'

'I don't know that the poor people of Norfolk would find Zeppelins rather wonderful after what they've been through,' his mother remarked.

'But I'm sure *this* one was just on reconnaissance.'

'Oh, you mean not actually bombing, but just looking for somewhere to drop 'em next time?' his father grunted.

'I'm surprised no one else heard it,' Freddie went on. 'As it was, I was out there in the garden on my own.' He paused, then added, 'All alone – apart from the beautiful and mysterious lady of the lake.'

His mother gave a peal of laughter. 'Freddie, you are too ridiculous!'

Freddie's eyes flickered up and locked briefly with Poppy's. 'What strange times we live in,' he murmured.

Chapter Five

The Spinney,
Mayfield

5th April 1915

My dearest girl,
Many thanks for your letter. I write with news of your
brother, who has at last stirred himself to answer
Kitchener's call. You may have heard of the Old Pals
units which have been formed to enable lads from the
same area to join up and fight together. Well, Billy has
enlisted with a dozen of his pals from the football club.
Between you and me, he could do little else after repeated
enquiries from all and sundry as to what he was doing to
help us win the war! He has gone for training in Watford,
and will come back here for a couple of days before being
posted. I will let you know any news. I am worried for

him, of course, but rather proud that he is prepared to fight for our country in her hour of need.

What an exciting trip you had to London to meet Miss Luttrell – and how generous of her to offer to make you an allowance if you become a VAD. I'd be so proud if you decided to do this! I am proud of you anyway, dearest child, so don't let me influence your decision. Whatever you think is best will be right.

Everyone wants to do their bit for their country now. At the factory we used to make cardboard boxes for tinned food, now we are making boxes for munitions. As I fold and seal them I think to myself that a Tommy in some foreign field will be handling this box soon. I am tempted to pop in an encouraging note or one of my homemade toffees!

Jane and Mary join me in sending all our best love and wishes for you to keep safe. Do let me know what you decide. On the back of this letter is Billy's address – I'm sure he'd love to hear from you.

Your loving mother

Poppy received the letter just before the servants got an unexpected summons to attend Mrs de Vere in the green drawing room and, thrilled that her brother had joined up, thought afterwards that it probably made some difference as to what she decided to do.

There were nine servants working at Airey House. Some years back, when both young ladies had been at home, there had been twenty-two, including a tutor and governess, but thirteen had now either gone off to fight or were doing war-related work. Those who remained had their own ideas about why they might have been called in to see Mrs de Vere, and expounded these as they went up the back stairs to the drawing room.

'We're going to have to put more hours in,' Joy, Mrs de Vere's personal maid, said. 'We've got half the number of servants here that we had two years ago so I reckon we're going to be asked to do two jobs!'

'No, I reckon they're going to reduce our pay and say it's to help the war effort,' said one of the valets. 'And then what they save will go in Old Man de Vere's back pocket.'

'Bet they shut up half the house and send most of us packing,' another said.

'I hope they don't stop us from having a bath on a Friday night!' said Poppy.

Outside the green drawing room, Cook and Joy jostled a little for position and then, in the absence of either butler or housekeeper, Cook knocked and was first through the door.

'I expect you're all terribly worried about your positions here,' Mrs de Vere began.

The more loyal of the servants said that they were and tried to look anxious, although the truth was that they were not too worried about losing their places because of the money that could be earned from other sorts of employment now.

'And I'm afraid I have to confirm your worst fears by saying that, sadly, Mr de Vere and I will not be needing many of you for very much longer. We're moving to our much smaller country house in Somerset. Here we'll be well away from the firing line, and be able to manage with minimum staff.'

Poppy waited, wondering if she was going to be part of that minimum staff. Surely Mrs de Vere would need a parlourmaid? On the other hand, now that even Billy had at last heard the call of his country, shouldn't she up and leave too?

'Begging your pardon, but when will you be going, ma'am?' asked Cook. 'Only, I've just ordered a jointed pig from the butcher to put in the ice house.'

'We'll be going as soon as we can get packed up – I hope by the end of May,' Mrs de Vere said. 'And I'm very pleased to tell you that this house will be taken over for the duration of the war as a cottage hospital for injured army officers.' She gave a faint smile. 'There's no ice house in our Somerset home, so we'll leave the officers the jointed pig with our compliments.'

The servants exchanged glances.

'That's me for bomb-making then,' Molly whispered to Poppy. 'I'll be helping the war effort *and* helping double my pay.'

Mrs de Vere went on, 'We will need a small core of staff, so I should like to retain Cook, my own maid Joy, and Poppy. Mr de Vere will still want George, of course – he still needs a valet.'

Poppy's heart gave a little jolt. She'd been half hoping that Mrs de Vere would say she didn't need any of her

Mayfield staff, then the decision about whether to apply for work as a VAD would have been made easier.

'If Cook, Joy and Poppy would stay behind for a moment, the rest of you can resume your duties until the end of the month,' Mrs de Vere said. 'You've all been most diligent and hard-working, and I shall be delighted to supply you with whatever references you require to obtain new positions.'

'I trust you'll be happy with me in the country, Poppy,' said Mrs de Vere, when the unwanted servants had left, muttering to themselves.

'Thank you, madam,' Poppy said uncertainly.

'As your duties will be a little more diverse, there may be an increase in your wage packet after a few months.' Mrs de Vere got up, walked to the window and scanned the skies. 'It's very quiet in Somerset, and we shall be able to keep out of the worst of the war. No Zeppelins there, at least!'

'No. Thank you, madam,' Poppy said. Then, rather unexpectedly, she found herself adding, 'But, do excuse me, unfortunately I won't be able to join you.'

'*What?*' Mrs de Vere turned, shocked. 'Why ever not?'

Poppy's heart was beating fast; she found herself almost as startled as Mrs de Vere. 'Because I've decided to take a voluntary position with the Red Cross.'

'Really?' Mrs de Vere said in astonishment. Cook and Joy turned to stare at her.

Poppy nodded. 'I hope to be trained in first aid and nursing.'

'I see. You've obviously looked into it.'

'Not really. I haven't even applied yet. It's just . . . I think I ought to do something to help the war effort.'

Mrs de Vere was not able to make the slightest objection to this. 'Very well,' she said, at last. 'I'll be sorry to lose you, Poppy, but you must do what you think right. If you wish to, you may stay on at Airey House while you make the necessary arrangements.'

'Thank you, madam.'

Poppy left the room and, feeling an urgent need to catch her breath, sat down on the back stairs for a moment and counted to ten very slowly. She was going to start something new and completely unknown. Once she'd left Airey House she might never see it or its occupants ever again. Any of them. Not even Freddie de Vere.

She counted ten deep breaths, allowing her thoughts to drift and settle. Leaving Airey House was the best thing she could do in so many ways, she told herself. She would be helping the war – and she would also be getting away from the absurd, dangerous, completely foolish way in which she had begun to regard Freddie de Vere.

'The bluebells are out in the woods,' Freddie said the next morning, catching Poppy on her own as she cleared away the breakfast things. 'Acres of them. I suppose you couldn't come for a . . .'

Shocked and pleased in equal measure, Poppy quickly shook her head. 'No, I couldn't possibly!'

'Unless you . . .'

But Mrs de Vere reappeared from the next room and Freddie went quiet while Poppy, blushing furiously, carried on clearing the table. No more was said, but that evening, on going to bed, she found a jam jar stuffed with bluebells outside her door.

Airey House
Mayfield
Herts

18ᵗʰ April 1915

Dear Miss Luttrell,
You'll be happy to hear that I've decided to take your advice about becoming a VAD and am writing to the address you gave me in London to request an interview. As you kindly suggested, I will give them your name as a referee, and Mrs de Vere said she would also supply me with a reference. The de Vere family have announced they are to leave Mayfield to live in Somerset for the duration of the war, so it has all worked out very well. Airey House is to become a hospital and convalescent home for officers.

I do hope I give a good interview at Devonshire House. I'll let you know as soon as I hear anything from them. I'm rather nervous and not at all sure that I'll be brave enough to face up to all the horrid things I might see, but I have been telling myself that if our boys are courageous enough to fight, then surely I ought to be courageous enough to care for them afterwards.

I did send (anonymously!) the white feather to the younger son, Freddie, and though it caused him acute embarrassment it hasn't made him join up. I've noticed him wearing a triangular brass badge lately – Cook says this is to show he is in a reserved occupation in case anyone tries to give him another feather.

With love and grateful thanks,

Poppy

It took several weeks for the interview to be arranged at Devonshire House and Poppy carried on working for the de Veres during this time. She wondered if someone might have told Freddie she was leaving, but didn't know for sure. The move to Somerset was taking longer than anyone had anticipated, with much furniture going into storage and members of the family travelling backwards and forwards to the country to take precious or delicate objects that couldn't be trusted to the removal men (or, a wartime novelty, removal *women*). Occasionally Poppy's path would cross with Freddie's, but they were never alone together and Poppy was beginning to think that she had imagined the night-time liaison on the lawn. When she thought that, she would smile wryly, for it had hardly been a *liaison* at all – they'd merely exchanged a couple of glances and almost held hands. Besides, he had an elegant, accomplished and beautiful young lady in his life. Who in their right mind would prefer a parlourmaid to the glowing Miss Cardew?

Poppy's preparations for her interview included looking through the book on home nursing that was kept in Cook's parlour, and reading the minute instructions on the bandages and antiseptic creams in the first-aid box. Unfortunately the nursing book was mainly about pregnancy and childbirth, so wasn't very useful, but she learned a little about pressure points and the importance of cleanliness from the instructions on the packets of bandages.

This scant knowledge did not give her much confidence, and by the time she got off the train at Euston and caught a bus towards Piccadilly Circus, she felt quite hollow with nerves. Twenty minutes later, wishing herself anywhere but there, she found herself going through the black and gold wrought-iron gates at Devonshire House.

There were two middle-aged matrons interviewing potential trainees for Voluntary Aid Detachments and they seemed nice enough. They were brisk and business-like, however, and when Poppy tried to make the smallest of light-hearted remarks about the awfulness of London traffic, they did not respond.

They wanted to know about Poppy's background and she told them that she'd been head girl and then won a college scholarship, but had been unable to take it up.

'Since leaving school I've been working for the de Vere family,' she explained. 'First in the kitchens and most lately as a parlourmaid.'

'Ah yes, the de Veres,' said the smaller, bird-like matron, as if she knew them.

'But *in service*,' said the other doubtfully.

'I expect that means you're probably very good at taking orders,' said her colleague.

Poppy nodded emphatically. 'Yes, I am.'

'But how do you intend to maintain yourself?' the first asked. 'You must be aware that the positions are voluntary.'

Poppy explained about her old schoolteacher's generous offer. They nodded and exchanged a word or two between themselves, but she couldn't hear what they were saying.

'And, Miss Pearson, what are your people doing to help the war effort?' the smaller matron asked.

Poppy was relieved that she could give the right answers. 'My father's dead, but my brother has recently begun training with a local division of the army and my mother works in a factory at night, making munition boxes.'

'And have you always wanted to be a nurse?'

Poppy bit her lip. 'To tell you the truth, I hardly thought that a girl like me with no medical background could do such a thing.' She took a breath. 'But then my old friend, the lady who is sponsoring me, told me that more and more nurses will be needed and that she thought I would be very suitable.'

'And have you ever undertaken any nursing duties?' asked the second matron, a solid woman with steel-grey hair in a bun.

'Well, I nursed my mother after childbirth,' Poppy replied. 'And if anyone in the de Vere family was ever ill, I helped tend to them. I know how to give a bed-bath . . . Oh, and when Mr de Vere had blood poisoning from getting his foot caught in a trap, I dressed the wound every morning.'

The first matron nodded; the other smiled. 'And are there any other ways in which you might be especially useful to us?'

'Well, I started work as a kitchen maid so I know how to keep a place spotless,' said Poppy. 'And I have excellent handwriting – everyone says so. I wondered if perhaps I might compose letters home for those soldiers who have broken arms or are temporarily blinded.'

'Temporarily or permanently . . .' said the bird-like matron drily, and Poppy remembered the horrific gas attacks which had recently blinded French and Canadian troops.

The second matron added, 'It may not always be nursing work you'll be called upon to do. You may be asked to serve departing troops with, say, two hundred cups of hot cocoa in half an hour. Do you think you could stay calm whilst coping with that sort of pressure?'

Poppy smiled. 'Excuse me, ma'am, but I'm used to serving a demanding family. I don't panic easily.'

The two matrons exchanged glances.

'Very good. Thank you, Miss Pearson, that will be all,' said the bird-like one. 'You will be hearing from us in due course.'

Poppy stood up and was about to curtsey when she

realised that it was no longer appropriate. She wasn't a parlourmaid any longer – she might possibly become a respected Red Cross nurse. She thanked both the matrons for seeing her and shook their hands.

On reaching Euston station after the interview, Poppy – more relaxed now – couldn't help but watch and sigh at some of the fond farewells and tearful scenes taking place on the concourse between Tommies and their sweethearts. After witnessing one girl run the length of the platform rather than let go of the hand of her khaki-clad beloved on the train, she was dabbing her eyes when someone touched her on the shoulder.

Startled, she wheeled round to come face to face with Freddie de Vere.

'Ah, I alarmed you,' he said. 'Do excuse me.'

'That's . . . that's quite all right,' Poppy managed to say, heart thudding and surprised almost out of her wits.

'Have you been lunching?'

Poppy hid a smile. She had only 'lunched' once in her life – when she'd met Miss Luttrell over a meat pie in the Corner House. 'No, I've been for an interview,' she said. 'I'm hoping to become a VAD.'

'Jolly commendable,' he said, nodding. 'In fact, I've been doing much the same.'

'You've applied to be a VAD?' she asked in surprise, although she knew that many men had signed on as orderlies and stretcher bearers.

He smiled and shook his head. 'No, I've been under-going interviews for a commission in the army. They're pretty desperate for recruits and so they've agreed to take me in the Officer Cadet Unit. I begin my training at Sandhurst on Monday.'

'Really? That's marvellous,' Poppy said, and she thought of the white feather and felt herself blush at the thought of what she'd done. As they crossed the concourse, she tried not to dwell on it.

'Kitchener has said that they need thirty-five thou-sand men to join up per week,' Freddie said. 'And of course we chaps don't like to be called cowards, and everyone thought that I really ought. Even Mother is happy that I'm going to fight the good fight.'

There was a slight catch to his voice and, with the new and strange chemistry between them, Poppy understood that he was frightened of what he might have to face. There was no shame in being scared, she wanted to say, and not everyone could feel brave all the time. But while she was trying to articulate the right words, he spoke again.

'You're catching the 3.12 back to Mayfield?' he said when they reached platform ten.

She nodded.

'Then perhaps we can travel together.'

Poppy's heart gave a skip – and then sank. She would be in his company for a little while longer, but what good would that do her? This whole flirtation business (for surely that was all it was) was silly and she was heading for a tremendous fall. Then she realised she was quite safe.

'No, I don't think we can,' she said, 'because I only have a third-class ticket.'

He pulled a small green oblong from his top pocket. 'And mine is . . . first class.'

Poppy nodded. That summed up all the differences between them in a nutshell.

He looked at her, smiled and continued walking along the platform. 'But I dare say the rail people would have no objection to my travelling in third!'

Poppy turned to him, unable to prevent a smile spreading across her face. 'I'm sure they wouldn't.'

'And we can talk about Zeppelins and maidens from the lake and all sorts of interesting things.'

'That would be . . .' *Wonderful, delightful, unbelievable* – but Poppy never finished the sentence, for there came a rapping on the window of one of the first-class carriages they were passing.

'Freddie! I say! Freddie de Vere!' A fur-hatted, middle-aged lady stared out, waved at Freddie and lowered her window. 'Freddie, dear, could you help me? I've some-how stuck my trunk in the door and I can't get in or out.'

'Oh. My Aunt Maud,' Freddie murmured to Poppy. 'I'm so sorry.'

Poppy, heart sinking, tried not to look crestfallen. 'That's quite all right. Of course you must go and help her.'

'I'll try and get away. But look,' he said urgently, 'if we don't get the opportunity to speak before I go, then I'll write to you from Sandhurst.'

'But I might not be at Airey House much longer.'

'Then leave a forwarding address!'

'I will,' Poppy said. 'And thank you for the bluebells . . .'

Freddie's Aunt Maud was looking rather troubled at the sight of him deep in conversation with a person of the lower classes. There was another sharp rap from the carriage window.

'Sorry. I'll have to . . .' Freddie leaped up the two steps into the first-class coach.

Poppy, as calmly as possible, continued walking down the platform towards the third class. She took a seat and, when the train pulled out, opened the magazine she'd bought – and didn't realise for half the journey that she was holding it upside down.

She put her head against the cool glass and wished she hadn't gone out to see the Zeppelin in the first place, wished he'd never looked at her *so* or spoken as he had, wished there was no such person as Miss Philippa Cardew. It didn't help, either, that a two-page spread in the magazine was given over to the changes there had been in society since the beginning of the war. Heiresses were now sweeping chimneys, housekeepers were mixing in high society, and lords were marrying laundry maids. Apparently anything was possible; the social barriers were crashing down all over Britain.

But, Poppy thought to herself, a certain rich young man could not forgo his aunt and his first-class seat to sit with a parlourmaid.

Chapter Six

As soon as the furniture and personal belongings of the de Vere family had been moved out of Airey House, the equipment needed to change it into a hospital and convalescent home for wounded officers had been moved in. Brand new hospitals were springing up all over the country and were urgently needed. Empty town halls, reclaimed asylums, schools, little used university buildings and many large private houses were being turned into temporary infirmaries. Some – like Airey House – were expressly for officers, while injured Tommies were being cared for in the largest buildings, in purpose-built 'hut hospitals' or in huge marquees specially erected in the grounds of existing infirmaries.

On a scorching day in June, one of the final deliveries of equipment, two van loads of hospital beds, had been delivered to Airey House and were now awaiting erection. Following this, the house would officially be taken over by the War Office. The few remaining members of the de Veres' staff, including Poppy and Molly, were due to leave the following morning and, as Poppy had not yet heard the result of her interview from Devonshire House, she'd arranged to go home and stay with her mother. If she was thought unsuitable to be a VAD, she would, she'd already decided, join Molly at one of the munitions factories. It would not be as thrilling or as useful as being a nurse, and she had heard that the chemicals turned your hair ginger, but at least she would be doing war work.

'Can you imagine it?' Molly said, as the two girls stood in what had once been the blue drawing room but was now empty of carpet, curtains, paintings and furniture. 'All down each side of this room will be beds: fourteen of them in a line! And there'll be as many beds again in the green drawing room and the dining room, and Cook's pantry will be a restroom for the nurses.'

'How long will they have the house for?' Poppy asked.

Molly shrugged. 'For the rest of the war, I suppose. The de Veres are just going to keep a few pieces of furniture and some suitcases of stuff in one of the cellar rooms.'

'What about upstairs?' Poppy asked. 'What will happen to the bedrooms?'

'Some of them will become treatment rooms,' said Molly, for she'd been chatting to one of the Tommies and knew all the latest, 'and Mrs de Vere's room is to become an operating theatre. They'll be setting broken bones and trying to put people back together in there.' She shivered dramatically. 'Bet that's not an easy task. I've heard that some of the men come back to Blighty near blown to bits or with no limbs at all.'

'I've heard that too,' Poppy said, and could not stop a picture forming in her mind of Freddie in a hospital bed with some superficial hurt which did not mar his handsome profile – while she, immaculate in her nurse's uniform, placed an ice pack on his brow.

Molly waved a hand in front of her face. 'Poppy, you've gone into a trance! I was asking you how your brother's getting on.'

Poppy pulled herself together. 'Oh, apparently – surprisingly – he's doing fairly well.'

'There you are!' Molly said.

'He wrote to Ma to say that he likes the fellows he's signed on with and enjoys the training sessions.'

Molly nodded. 'Well, they do say that war brings out the best in people.'

'He told me that they've all promised to look out for each other if they get involved in a skirmish.' Poppy was silent for a moment, then said, 'How strange it all is. The war has changed everything, hasn't it? This house, our jobs, our families, our homes.'

'Mmm. I s'pose it has.'

'Do you think it's true that because everyone is pulling together, all the different classes will sort of merge into one?'

'Eh?' Molly looked at her, puzzled. 'How d'you mean?'

Poppy made several starts at formulating what she wanted to say without mentioning Freddie and herself and any potential relationship, but found it too much of a struggle. 'Oh . . . nothing,' she said finally. 'I was just being silly.'

'Just think, Mr Jessop the butler is in Boulogne now!' Molly said, hardly noticing Poppy's struggle. 'He's helping feed hundreds of soldiers as they pass through on their way to fight.'

'Wouldn't it be strange if he served Mr Jasper,' Poppy said, for Jasper de Vere was due to receive his first posting at the end of June and was hoping to see active service in France as soon as possible.

A little later, Poppy made a pot of tea for the team of Tommies who were putting up the beds and, taking it in to them, smiled to hear them complain that they were doing women's work.

'Making up beds for officers! We'll be plumping their pillows next,' one soldier said.

'And giving 'em a goodnight kiss!' said his pal.

'I never signed up for this,' said the first.

'Nor did I! I signed up to get my hands on Fritz.' He balled his fist hard into his palm and imitated the noise of a bomb going off. 'I'd show 'em. Just let me get at the blighters!'

'Knowing our luck, we'll probably spend the whole blimmin' war in Blighty.'

'Fat lot of good to anyone, that'll be!'

Their sergeant major entered the room. 'But at least you'll be alive and not under the Flanders mud,' he said. 'Now cut the cackle and get on with the job.'

Poppy, still smiling, went back into the kitchen, where Molly was holding out an envelope with *Devonshire House* printed in the top-left corner.

'The postman just brought this for you!' she said excitedly. 'What do you think? Yes or no?'

'No,' said Poppy, fearing the worst.

Molly pushed the letter at her. 'Quickly, then. Open it and see!'

The Recruitment Office,
Devonshire House,
London SW1

13th June 1915

Dear Miss Pearson,
Following your interview at this office, we are pleased to inform you that the Voluntary Aid Detachment of the Red Cross will be able to offer you training in general war work, including first aid and nursing.

Please attend this office on 15th June at two o'clock, when you will be assigned lodgings. Training will commence the following day.
Yours truly,

For Voluntary Aid Detachment

That evening, Poppy walked over to see her mother and tell her the good news, then, having received a note from Miss Luttrell to say she would be spending several nights that week back at Mayfield, called in there to show her the letter too.

'My congratulations, dear,' Miss Luttrell said, kissing her on each cheek. 'I knew they'd want you. Now you're *really* going to help our boys!'

Poppy nodded excitedly, still hardly believing that she'd been accepted.

Miss Luttrell made a pot of tea. 'You're going to find yourself living and working amongst all sorts of people,' she said, pouring it out, 'and most of them will be well-to-do. I want to warn you against making up stories about your background – you might come unstuck. Just stay true to yourself.'

Poppy listened and nodded, waiting for an opportunity to speak to Miss Luttrell about something in particular. When there was a lull in the conversation, she seized the moment. 'The younger de Vere boy, Freddie, has also signed up now,' she said.

Miss Luttrell raised her eyebrows. 'Excellent. I should think so!'

'I sent him the feather,' Poppy said. 'But I don't know if that was the reason he enlisted.'

'Not the feather on its own perhaps, but he'll have been getting a certain amount of pushing from those around him. Anyway, it's not before time – it's rumoured that the War Office will begin conscription early next year, so all those cowardly so-and-sos who've refused to fight for their country will be made to!'

Poppy hesitated. The something which she wanted to speak to Miss Luttrell about was the same something she'd tried to bring up with Molly. She made several false starts and then began again rather timidly, 'Miss Luttrell, I keep reading that a woman's role in the world is changing. They say that because we're managing to hold down men's jobs – important jobs – we'll probably get the vote when the war ends and . . .' her voice trailed away and Miss Luttrell looked at her expectantly, '. . . and you did say that the war will *level* people.'

'Yes, dear, I did. So?'

'So does that mean . . . Do you also think it's possible that young men from good families will now keep company with girls who might once have been thought of as below them?'

Miss Luttrell looked at her keenly. 'Possibly,' she said, 'but you must remember that these young officers want to . . .' she gave a delicate cough, '. . . *keep company* for one specific reason. And that reason is not marriage.'

Poppy felt her cheeks begin to turn warm.

'There is a certain desperation in young men who are going to war – oh, I know how it was for my generation during the Boer War! Men and women can get together for the wrong reasons.' She grasped Poppy's hand. 'Be sensible. Don't listen to a plea from a young man that you should consummate your relationship in case he

61

dies at the front. If you do, you could find yourself with more than you bargained for at the end of the war.'

On Poppy falling silent, Miss Luttrell added, 'You do know what I mean, don't you, dear?'

Poppy nodded. She knew what Miss Luttrell was alluding to, but she and Freddie hadn't even kissed! It sowed a little seed of doubt in her mind, however. *A certain desperation in young men who are going to war . . .* was *that* why Freddie was paying her so much attention?

Chapter Seven

Poppy was greeted at the door of Devonshire House by a girl in army uniform, who scrutinised the letter Poppy handed her and directed her to a waiting area just off a large, tiled hall. Here she sat on a bench with perhaps twenty other girls, all with suitcases and bags at their feet, all anxiously waiting to hear what they were going to be doing and where they'd be sleeping that night. Several of them were already speaking in low voices, comparing notes, talking about their homes or saying how much they missed their sweethearts who'd gone to fight. There was a kind of status battle going on, Poppy realised, with those who had brothers or fiancés at the front scoring the most points. She could not help noticing, either, that most of the young women had expensive leather luggage, were very well dressed and spoke in what her mother called 'cut-glass accents'. She would be working alongside the type of girl she'd been calling 'madam' and curtseying to just a few weeks before – how odd that would be.

After a few moments of staring at the floor, Poppy found a little confidence and began to look around her, wondering whether she would be billeted with any of these girls, hoping that they would be friendly, wondering what they would be like to work with. Those who'd removed their gloves were showing awfully pale and un-workaday hands!

Four names were called out and four girls picked up their luggage and went into the next room, never to be seen by Poppy again. More time went by. Young women in different uniforms went backwards and forwards carrying paperwork, tea was served to the waiting girls from a trolley, further names were called and more new girls arrived to take the places of those who'd disappeared into other rooms. Another bench was brought in so that by the time someone called 'Miss Pearson, please' there were new recruits seated right around the four walls of the waiting area.

Poppy got up, tapped at the door and went in, no longer nervous, just grateful that they had called her.

'You are Poppy Pearson?' the matron asked.

Poppy nodded. 'Yes, madam.'

'Well, Pearson, as a VAD you will always be known by your surname,' came the response. She scanned the form she had before her, then peered over her glasses at Poppy. 'You have no formal first-aid knowledge?'

'No, madam.'

'But I see here that nursing is the area in which you want to work, rather than office work or driving?'

'It is, madam.'

'I want to emphasise straight away that you may not get the opportunity of work in France or Belgium. Only the crème de la crème of our nursing VADs will have the great honour of working alongside our fighting men.'

'Thank you, madam, but I wasn't considering asking to work abroad,' Poppy said, thinking that nursing in this country was going to be quite difficult enough.

'Very well. As to your duties: you may be asked to scrub the floor of a ward, to roll bandages, to clean equipment, to wash windows or clear up after someone who has lost control of their bodily functions.'

Poppy nodded. So far, so much what she was used to.

'You must be ever willing to help and never complain at any task you might be given. The army rule of obey first and complain afterwards should always be uppermost in your mind, and as we *are* a military detachment you will be subject to discipline similar to that in the British Army. You will wear your nurse's uniform at all times and make sure it's immaculate, address all your superiors as sir or madam, stand to attention when spoken to by an officer and keep your temper whatever the provocation. You will undertake the smallest detail ordered by a superior and draw yourself to attention whenever the national anthem is played.'

'Of course, madam,' Poppy said, trying not to look too overwhelmed by all these demands. 'I've been a parlourmaid in a big house for four years and that's been good training. I'm used to hard work and obeying orders.'

'Then you're halfway there, Pearson,' said the matron. 'VADs are part nurse and part kitchen maid. From what you've told me, I take it that you won't need training in how to scrub a floor or serve tea, like some of our new young lady volunteers.'

Poppy shook her head, hiding a smile.

'You'll be learning all sorts of tasks whilst you're training, but it'll be up to each individual nursing sister as to which you'll be allowed to practise on the wards. You may be called upon to live in a tent, a hostel or in lodgings, and after eight weeks' training in a variety of things you may be sent anywhere in the country.'

'Very good, madam,' Poppy said.

'Now, Pearson, where shall we put you?' Several moments went by whilst the matron consulted her paperwork. 'Southampton again, I think,' she said eventually. 'It's the first port of call for injured soldiers coming back from the front line, and at the moment they need as many girls down there as they can get. You'll be staying at what was the Young Women's Christian Association Hostel. How does that sound?'

'That sounds very good, thank you, madam,' said Poppy. At least it wasn't a tent.

'So, if you're ready to go now, ask at the travel office through the door . . .' she gestured to the right, '. . . and they'll supply you with a warrant to catch the afternoon train.'

VAD Unit No. 1765
c/o YWCA Hostel, Southampton

16ᵗʰ June 1915

Hello Billy,
I expect Ma has told you: I have enrolled as a VAD and I am on my way to Southampton on the train as I write this. My unit number is written above. If you want to write to me then please address letters to me c/o the YWCA Hostel.

I'm terrifically proud to be helping the war effort and I expect you are, too. You must have nearly finished your training. I wonder if you will be posted abroad? Ma said that you are with a group of pals – I expect that will make all the difference and stop you feeling homesick. Billy, please make sure you write to Ma regularly and let her know (as far as you are allowed to by the censor) where you are and that you are well, for she will be worrying about you very much. Let's hope that before too long we win the war and are back living peacefully in Mayfield.

I said I'm proud to be doing what I'm doing, but I'm also very nervous. I know my life won't be in danger like yours, but I'll be away from everyone I know and doing a difficult job whilst trying to keep a smile on my face no matter what. Southampton could be South America as far as I'm concerned – I won't know anyone and everyone says the VADs are mostly very posh. Think of me speaking in my best voice all the time – it will be such a strain!

Writing of Mayfield, Ma told me that because of the anti-German feeling, Mrs Schmit had to close her sweet shop. Such a shame – she was a nice lady and had never even lived in Germany! People shouted at her in the street, though, and twice her front window was kicked in.

Do let me know how things are going.
With best love,

your sister Poppy

She wrote a few lines to her mother and sent postcards to both Molly and Cook, telling them where she was going and asking that any letters be sent on to the YWCA in Southampton. And then she just stared out of the window while the train belched steam and the English countryside passed by. Both she and Billy in uniform, she marvelled. How quickly things had changed!

Southampton. First port of call for injured soldiers. She didn't want to see Freddie injured – couldn't bear to think of it – but if he was, she would be there waiting for him . . .

Chapter Eight

B y the time Poppy arrived at what had once been the YWCA Hostel in the back streets of Southampton, it was late in the afternoon. The big house was shabby and had an interior which was quite cheerless, but it was placed very conveniently for the VADs at local military hospitals.

The new girls were allocated a bed space as they arrived at the hostel, and Poppy found herself in a largish room which had been partitioned off by faded curtains into three separate areas. One of these areas was already occupied, to judge by the overflowing locker and the clothes hanging behind the bed, so she took one of the other two cubicles, which had its own small window. She sat down on the narrow bed and, before unpacking, closed her eyes and took several deep breaths to compose herself.

She was here. She had arrived. She was going to be a nurse . . .

On the third breath there was a sudden noise outside her curtain, the thump and clatter of cases being thrown down and the stamp of a foot.

'Oh, how perfectly hateful!' Poppy heard a girl's voice say. 'I can't bear to be confined in such an awful dank little space!'

The curtain which surrounded Poppy was tugged open a little and a face looked in.

'I say, *you've* got a window!' said the girl. She pulled the curtain aside and Poppy saw a tall, slim young woman of about eighteen, in a dark linen coat and velvet hat, her fair hair flowing in ripples down her back.

'I just got here and took . . .' Poppy began.

The girl sighed. 'Do you mean that if I'd been five minutes earlier I could have had *this* space instead? With the window?'

Poppy, used to giving way before authority, shrugged. 'I really don't mind not having a window. Would you like to take this bed?'

'Oh, how absolutely *sweet* of you!' The girl picked up her case and beauty box and was through the curtain before Poppy could change her mind. 'My name's Beatrice Jameson. I understand we are to be known by our second names. What's yours?'

'Pearson. Poppy Pearson,' said Poppy, and the two girls shook hands.

'It's most awfully decent of you, Pearson,' Jameson said. 'Thank you so much! I'm absolutely claustrophobic, you see. I can't bear to be confined in a small space.'

'That's all right . . . Jameson.'

The two girls looked around them: at the paint flaking from the window frames and the almost threadbare curtains.

'Rather shabby, isn't it?' Jameson said. 'One couldn't say that they've gone to a lot of trouble preparing for us.'

Poppy shrugged again. 'I suppose all the trouble has gone on improving the hospitals.'

'Oh, of course!' Jameson cried, instantly contrite. 'Our boys must have the very best of everything.' She smiled. 'I can't wait to begin nursing, can you? *Such* a privilege.' She began to remove her gloves. 'Do you have a sweetheart who's gone to fight?'

'Not exactly,' Poppy replied and, thinking of Freddie de Vere, couldn't resist adding, 'but there is someone I'm awfully fond of who's undergoing his training at the moment.'

'I have two brothers fighting in Flanders.'

Poppy remembered Billy and added hastily, 'My brother is undergoing military training at the moment.'

'Oh, this war is simply frightful,' Jameson said. 'Just this week I discovered that a very dear friend of mine has lost her husband.'

'How terribly sad,' Poppy murmured.

'Quite. It seems that a girl only has to announce that she's getting married these days for a telegram to appear saying that her fiancé is dead.'

Poppy couldn't think of what to say to this, and there was a moment's pause in the conversation before Jameson said rather pointedly, 'But now, if you wouldn't mind excusing me, I think I'll unpack my clothes and have a bath.'

'Of course,' said Poppy, and she jumped up from the bed, took her case and went into the next cubicle to begin her own unpacking.

Once she'd hung her clothes on hooks and filled the locker with her bits and pieces, there was nothing to do but sit on the little school chair she'd been provided with and wait for something to happen – for some official to claim her, perhaps.

She got out her notepad and pen and wrote to Miss Luttrell, giving her address in Southampton and saying how nervous and excited she was. Whilst she was doing this, Jameson disappeared from her cubicle for some considerable time and arrived back in a waft of talcum powder and a white negligee. Poppy heard the bed springs creak as she flung herself down, then came silence, so it appeared that she had fallen asleep. Outside in the hallway, Poppy heard the occasional footsteps echoing as a girl went up or down the stairs, but apart from that there was hardly any noise from within the building. All the VADs who lived there, Poppy supposed, must be at work at their various hospitals.

Some moments later, Poppy was doing what she normally did when she had nothing to do – thinking of

Freddie – when suddenly there was a noise on the stairway and two girls came into the room.

'It's too bad, really it is!' one girl was saying. 'Too absolutely selfish.'

'Everyone knows it's your turn for first bath water!' said the other.

'Unless . . .'

There was a small gap where the curtains around Poppy's bed didn't meet, and she looked through this to see two young women in nurse's uniform making gestures towards the curtaining which enclosed her and Jameson.

'Unless someone new has arrived . . .' the other one said.

Poppy leaned forward to tug at her curtain, reveal herself and say hello.

The two girls looked at her severely. 'Is it you who's used all the bath water?' said the first of the girls, who was a few years older than Poppy, had short dark hair and hazel eyes.

Poppy shook her head. 'I haven't actually *seen* a bathroom yet.'

'Well, someone has,' the girl said, 'and the whole hostel knows that it's my turn to have the first bath this week. I've been working for twelve hours without a break!'

'Oh dear,' said Poppy.

'The selfish beast must have had it absolutely *brimming* with water,' said the same girl. 'The orderly says there's not a drop left in the hot tank.'

'It smells like a tart's boudoir in there, too!' said the other girl.

There was a creak from the bed in Jameson's cubicle and the cross girl wheeled round. 'Are there two of you?' she asked Poppy. 'Two new girls?'

On Poppy nodding, the other girl tugged at the curtain and Jameson was revealed, stretched out on her bed and looking guilty.

'Did you take all the bath water?' the girl demanded.

Jameson, in pristine white ruffles, looked alarmed. 'I didn't realise. I'm most awfully sorry!' she said. 'Someone always draws me a bath before supper and –'

'Not here they don't,' came the retort. 'Here you take your turn and once a month, if you're lucky, you'll be in the first five to have a bath and get two inches of hot water. The rest of the time you have to line up and get one inch of lukewarm water, and if some selfish beast has got there before you and taken it all, you get nothing.'

Jameson said over and over how dreadfully, *terribly* sorry she was, but it took a considerable amount of grovelling on her part (and she was probably not much used to that, Poppy thought) before the other girl was placated. She and Jameson then had to sit through a short lecture about how many hours the VAD, whose name was Moffat, had been on her feet, how she hadn't stopped for as much as a sandwich, and how Jameson should have asked the orderly if it was all right for her to bathe when she wasn't even on the rota and therefore had no rights whatsoever.

Poppy, thanking the Lord that she hadn't felt the need for a bath, listened to this in silence. Jameson did, too, for this was a real-life VAD they were being lectured by, in a crumpled grubby apron which looked as if it had seen nursing action and with a red cross on her bib which meant, as far as most of the world was concerned, that she was a heroine. Poppy gazed at her admiringly, knowing that the next morning, she'd be taking the first steps towards joining those hallowed ranks.

Supper, a bowl of soup in the canteen, came next. Poppy was pleased when Moffat joined them, for she'd feared she might have been lumped in with Jameson as another selfish beast. Moffat, however, did not seem to hold grudges and began telling stories about life as a VAD – she'd joined up right at the start of the war – before, yawning profusely, she excused herself to go to bed.

Poppy was tired, but when she went upstairs she found it difficult to sleep, and worries about new responsibilities competed with thoughts of Freddie de Vere. Did he ever think of her? Would he write to her as he'd promised? Was the lady of the lake a very lovely thing?

With a sigh she realised that if Freddie were awake, his thoughts were probably all of the war and fighting and death, for she didn't think it very likely that soldiers had much time or energy to think about love. Nevertheless, she could not shake off the attractive notion that she and Freddie were meant to be together . . .

*

The following morning at seven thirty, Poppy, plus Jameson and ten other new VADs, were met in the dusty lounge of the hostel by Sister Malcolm, who told them that she was going to oversee their training. A list of rules and regulations was produced: VADs were to act with decorum at all times, there was to be no fraternising with officers, no going out dancing, and the integrity of the profession was to be upheld at all times. There should be no going out and about in ordinary clothes.

'Besides, you will probably find that wearing your uniform gives you status and brings certain privileges,' Sister told them. 'Free cinema tickets, for instance, and cheap meals. I often find that when a cab driver sees that I'm a nurse, he will refuse to take any fare from me.'

A basic uniform for each girl was produced: a blue cotton dress and white apron with that all-important red cross.

'Some of these garments have been worn before,' said Sister Malcolm, 'so I'm also giving each of you a pattern so that you can make a uniform in your own size when you have time. Please don't be tempted to add your own little touches: any jewellery, ribbons or other adorn-ments, either to your uniform or outer clothes, will be frowned on.' She walked between the girls, studying their faces. 'Some of the ward sisters are very strict about make-up. I've known girls to be sent home for having the tiniest smudge of colour on their lips.' She paused by one girl. 'I suppose that is a natural pink on your cheeks?'

'Yes, sister,' said the girl, but when Sister had moved on, Poppy saw her scrubbing at her cheeks with a hanky.

'A sister's word is law at all times,' continued Sister Malcolm. 'Never talk back, or undermine her, or – heaven help us! – a *matron's* instructions, or you'll find yourself heading straight for home on the next train. In the unlikely event that you're allowed into a ward before your training is up . . .'

There was a murmur of disappointment from the girls.

'What?' said Sister in mock surprise. 'Did you think you'd be let loose on our injured boys immediately? Did you picture yourselves setting broken bones, bandaging sore heads and saving lives?'

The girls smiled sheepishly. They all had, of course.

'As I said, in the unlikely event that you find yourself in a ward and come face to face with an injured man, you will take your cue from the ward sister. She will understand her patient and know if he should be asleep or awake, whether she must be brisk or gentle with him, if he is able to eat or drink. You may not so much as touch a patient without her express permission. Each ward sister will have her own rules and regulations, her own way of doing things, and you must be guided by her at all times. Do you understand?'

The girls nodded solemnly.

'Are there any questions?'

Jameson put up her hand. 'Are there . . . will we see some terribly gruesome sights?'

'Yes, you will,' said Sister Malcolm. 'Next?'

The new VADs were allocated their first tasks. Poppy and four other girls were asked to clear the top floor of the hostel of an amount of old furniture, and collect and assemble four beds ready to be occupied by new VADs. Two girls were given the task of rolling bandages; others were set variously to scrub floors in an army canteen, sterilise operating equipment at a nearby military hospital or attend their first nursing and first-aid course. Apart from the latter, these tasks were perhaps not what the girls had hoped they would be doing, but everyone tried to look willing – whilst hoping against hope that the time would go swiftly until they could begin to do what they'd joined up for: to care for injured soldiers.

Chapter Nine

Roughly halfway through Poppy's training period, Sister Malcolm arrived earlier than usual at the hostel, looking rather anxious.

'One of the senior sisters has got a bad bout of influenza and I've been asked to join a hospital train taking a large group of wounded men from the docks,' she said. 'An orderly will be along to take over from me here this morning and he'll be able to deal with any queries you might have. In the meantime . . .' her eyes quickly scanned the dozen girls, 'I need two girls who are used to following orders – girls who can obey instructions without question.'

She looked across the girls and Poppy drew herself up, feeling as if she were at school and hoping to be chosen for the end-of-term play. After a moment's consideration, Sister Malcolm reached out to touch Poppy's shoulder and that of the girl behind her.

'Pearson, is it? And Matthews. Go upstairs for your

outdoor clothes, put them on as swiftly as possible and come back down.'

Poppy, pleased she had been paired with Matthews, a giggly, curly-haired girl from the same sort of background as herself, ran up the stairs as quickly as her long skirts and starched pinafore would allow and put on her outdoor outfit. This had only just been distributed and consisted of a smart dark navy coat with red facings on the collar and cuffs, and a navy blue straw hat. The all-important band bearing a red cross was worn on the left arm. There was no mirror but she looked at her reflection in the window in Jameson's cubicle and was startled at what she saw: she actually looked like a real nurse. She, Poppy Pearson, was going to help wounded men straight from the front line, newly arrived at the docks.

Jameson arrived upstairs just as Poppy was going down, and seemed rather surprised at the sight of her. 'I must say that navy blue suits your hair,' she said. 'And I do rather envy you going on a hospital train.'

'I just hope I don't do anything majorly daft,' Poppy said.

'Well, you're not exactly going to find yourself sewing up head wounds or conducting operations, are you?' Jameson said with a yawn, for she still hadn't got used to early rising. 'Sister just wanted a couple of girls who were used to hard graft.'

'That's certainly me,' Poppy said drily.

'You'll probably just be washing out the lavs.'

'I dare say.' Poppy hid a smile as she spoke, thinking that no one, even the tactless Jameson, could take away the thrill of being one of the first two girls in the detachment to be asked to do *real* war work.

Downstairs, Matthews and Poppy exchanged comments about how nervous they were, until they heard a call from outside of 'Girls! Now, please!' from Sister Malcolm, and hurried out to where an old army pick-up truck was waiting in the street. There was a regular soldier in the driver's seat, and Sister was sitting beside him.

'Quick as you can!' she called.

Both girls clambered in, ignoring the appreciative wink from the Tommy.

'Any more coming?' he asked jovially.

'No, just we three,' said Sister Malcolm.

'Pity,' he said. 'Any more and you might have had to sit on my lap, sister!'

Matthews nudged Poppy and she giggled before she could stop herself, but Sister Malcolm acted as if she hadn't heard and was very icy with him for the short drive to Southampton station, murmuring, 'Such insolence!' under her breath as his truck drove away. She left both the girls waiting under the station clock whilst she dashed off to discover which train they were needed on.

The concourse was chaotic, heaving with Tommies, officers, equipment and kitbags nearly as big as their owners. There were two train loads of new troops waiting to catch their ships, cross the Channel and join the fighting, as well as several hundred wounded men newly arrived from France and waiting to be despatched to hospitals all over England. Along with the soldiers, there was a crowd of townspeople waiting to see off one group and welcome home another.

'So many people. So many soldiers!' Poppy gasped.

Matthews said, 'Well, the front line goes along four hundred miles.'

'You can tell which boys are going to fight and which are coming back, can't you?' said Poppy, for the new boys had spruce uniforms and were jaunty and smiling, occasionally bursting into song or whistling cheerily, whereas those returning, apart from any obvious wounds, were tired and grey of face, with muddy, bloody uniforms. They might have looked awfully weary, but they didn't look miserable, for they were back in Blighty and out of the war.

'So many of them coming and going,' Poppy mused. 'Who actually decides where the injured ones should end up? Do you know?'

'Well, my big sister's a VAD at a hospital in Dover,' Matthews said. 'She told me that they assess the injured lads when they come in from the battlefield, and if they're bad enough they get what they call a "Blighty ticket" and come back on the first ship. Some of these boys go to the local hospitals at the port they arrive at, particularly the really badly injured, because they might not survive a railway journey. Some get taken to London or one of the other big cities – anywhere they've got the space, and close to their families if possible.' She sighed, and added in a low voice, 'Some die on the journey over, of course . . .'

Poppy was about to ask something else, but Sister Malcolm was gesturing to them from across the concourse. 'Pearson, Matthews!' she called. 'Come with me.'

She led the way to a platform where a long train waited, steam already belching out of its funnel and the red crosses on its sides showing that it was a hospital train and, as such, should not be attacked by the enemy or harmed in any way. As they walked along beside it, Poppy looked through the windows and was both gripped and appalled to see that the train had been converted and, instead of seats, a lot of the carriages contained what looked like narrow bunk beds, or racks to hold stretchers. One carriage was completely closed off, its blinds rolled down all the way along.

'That's a small operating theatre,' Sister Malcolm said as they passed it. 'Some poor chaps are bound to need stitching or warrant some other urgent attention before we get to Manchester.'

'Manchester!' Poppy said.

Sister Malcolm nodded. 'Though we'll see next to nothing of it. We'll get there, the boys will be taken off and our train will be loaded with supplies for our return to Southampton.'

They passed another, smaller carriage with its blinds down, which Sister said was for men with facial injuries.

'They don't want to be stared at as we go through stations.'

'Where will *they* be going, then?' Matthews asked.

'To one of the hospitals which specialise in help-ing men with that sort of injury,' Sister Malcolm said. 'They can rebuild noses and jaws and make false ears and so on. In fact, you'd be surprised at what they can do these days. The boys call them the tin noses shops.'

Poppy and Matthews smiled, though Poppy thought it was one of the most tragic things she'd ever heard. Tin noses, tin ears, tin masks . . . How could anyone manage to live their life wearing a tin face?

Almost at the end of the train, the little group came to a carriage which had been transformed into a buffet car, with a counter running most of its length and what appeared to be a long, narrow kitchen behind it.

Sister Malcolm halted. 'This is where you two girls will be for the next few hours.'

'Working in the buffet?' Poppy asked.

'Yes indeed. The boys who are "up" patients – that is, those well enough to be on their feet – will come along here and queue for their cheese rolls and tea. Those who are confined to their bunks will be served by orderlies, who'll come along with trays.'

'And we'll be handing out the food?' Poppy asked, secretly thrilled at the thought of greeting, being ter-ribly nice to and – who knew? – maybe even flirting a little with scores of young Tommies.

'No, I'm afraid you'll be slicing rolls,' Sister said. 'Slicing, buttering and putting a chunk of cheese inside, then passing them through the hatch to whoever is running the show. You'll also be seeing that the tea and cocoa doesn't run out.'

'Who'll actually be serving them, then?' Matthews asked, while Poppy tried not to look too disappointed.

Sister smiled. 'Your time will come,' she said, 'but today it's the turn of more experienced VADs who've earned that privilege. Also, we try and break you new girls in gently to the realities of the injuries you might see. There will be boys with limbs missing, those who are blinded or who have gangrenous or open wounds. Some of them, trust me, are not pretty sights. You'll be in the back of the kitchen and at a distance today, and I hope that you'll both be sensible enough not to react badly if you see anything which alarms you.'

Poppy and Matthews both assured her that they would try not to let her down.

'If you do happen to meet a badly injured man, the best thing you can do is bid him welcome home and give him a smile. Some of these men haven't seen a girl for months and you'd be surprised at how a pleasant greeting from a girl their own age can help them feel human again.'

'Where will you be, Sister?' Poppy asked as the three of them climbed aboard and hung up their coats and hats.

'I shall be with two doctors and half a dozen nurses and we'll be going from the front to the back of the train, sterilising, stitching, tidying and bandaging as we go. The doctors on board will assess everyone and will hope to have seen them all by the time we reach our destination. It means we can be much more efficient at the other end.'

Along the counter of the narrow kitchen were six huge baskets each containing a couple of hundred fresh rolls. There was also an urn of water, just coming to the boil, and a vast pottery bowl containing a soft mass of margarine.

'The boys will have their own enamel cups and plates, and you'll find knives and spoons . . .' she looked around, '. . . somewhere or other.' She smiled at them. 'I must go and find my team. Get a message to me if you're in difficulty. Otherwise, Pearson and Matthews, work well and I'll see you both later.'

She disappeared and the two girls looked at each other.

'I need to practise something,' Poppy said.

'What's that?'

'Saying, "Welcome home, soldier" without blubbing.'

The two VADS who would be serving the boys arrived: Rees and Colebrook, who turned out to be very friendly and capable. They'd both done hospital runs before and said that the amount of food that the Tommies could put away was impressive.

'They're allowed two rolls – great crusty things that I'd struggle to eat half of,' said Rees, who was plump and smiley.

'If they want to queue up again, they're allowed another roll,' put in Colebrook.

'And another – for as long as they last,' added Rees. 'Some of the poor darlings haven't eaten for twenty-four hours.'

There was a huge metal teapot standing by, which the two VADs said held about fifty cups.

'But you'd better not brew up yet,' Rees said, 'in case it gets stewed.'

'Our boys don't like stewed tea!' added Colebrook.

'We'd better get started on our roll mountain instead then,' said Matthews, and she and Poppy went behind the partition to begin the slicing and buttering.

They had only got through about a quarter of the rolls when they heard clapping and cheering from further down the platform.

Colebrook put her head round the serving hatch to speak to them. 'The boys are coming on board! Come and see.'

All four girls went to the open door of the carriage and leaned out, two standing on the top step and two on the one below. Seagulls cried overhead, a band could be heard playing on the concourse, and there was much flag waving and shouting from the crowd who'd gathered.

The funnels of the docked troopships could just be seen, and it was from this direction that they came, stretcher cases first, then the 'walking wounded', two by two in a long line, some walking quite briskly but with injuries to their arms, some limping, others leaning on crutches or being helped along by willing orderlies. The stretcher cases mostly boarded the train further down, but as the raggle-taggle line of men came closer to the buffet car and Poppy saw a couple of lads who'd been blinded being led by their companions, she could feel her nose prickling and a lump forming in her throat.

She quickly went back into the kitchen, followed by Matthews.

'I don't want to stay out there in case I make a chump of myself,' Poppy said.

'Me neither.' Matthews gulped.

Rees and Colebrook came in as well.

'It always gets me,' Colebrook said.

'I think we're being very wise.' Rees blew her nose heartily. 'The last thing those boys need is a pack of girls blubbing all over them.'

Fifteen minutes later, with men laid out on every bunk and squeezed into every corner, the train chugged out of its siding, bellowing steam, for the cross-country journey across country to Manchester. As Sister Malcolm had predicted, the minute it left the station there were boys queuing for food, and it seemed that as soon as they'd eaten their rolls they began to queue for more, so that Nurse Rees had to tell them with mock sternness that there would be no seconds until every man on board had had his firsts. Even so, the demand was incessant: several times queues built up because Poppy and Matthews couldn't slice and butter quickly enough, and they heard much light-hearted banter between Rees, Colebrook and the men about how they'd thought they might die of their wounds, but never thought they'd die for want of a bread roll. Poppy and Matthews – buttering for England, they declared – marvelled at the resilience of the men, laughed at the jokes and occasionally, if the soldier had a nice voice, turned and peeped through the hatch to see his face.

The train made three stops at major stations, one for a full hour. Here three St John nurses boarded the train and went from front to back distributing treats for the men: cigarettes, pipe tobacco, newspapers, and postcards so that they could write to their families and let them know what had happened to them. At the second stop a vast assortment of cakes was put on board – every local woman had given up her egg-and-sugar allowance for a week so that she could bake a cake for a Tommy.

The following stop was scheduled to be thirty minutes and several of the injured soldiers, wanting to stretch their legs, got off the train to walk up and down the length of the platform.

Poppy glanced out of the carriage window, then gasped and looked again more closely. It looked like . . . yes . . . it really *was* Jasper de Vere, his khaki trousers cut away to show a heavily bandaged foot and leg, limping along the platform leaning on a crutch.

Jasper *injured*, she thought, appalled. He could only have been in France a month!

She approached Rees, her heart pounding. 'I say, I think I've just seen someone I know,' she said. 'Do you think I could possibly go and have a word?'

'Oh, I think we could spare you for a few moments,' Rees said. 'What do you reckon, Colebrook?'

'I think that would be absolutely fine,' said the other VAD.

Poppy carefully climbed off the train and approached Jasper de Vere, pleased she was seeing him whilst she was dressed as a nurse. Maybe she couldn't help hoping, he would tell Freddie that he'd seen her. Maybe he would even have news of Freddie?

'Mr de Vere?' she said tremulously.

He turned in surprise, but didn't seem to recognise her.

'It's Poppy. From Airey House,' she said, but he just continued looking at her and frowning. 'I was the parlourmaid, sir,' she said in a whisper.

'Oh, my dear girl, of course,' he said. 'Do excuse me.' He nodded at her approvingly. 'You make a jolly fine-looking nurse, if you don't mind me saying.'

'Thank you, sir. But you've been injured!' she said, and immediately thought to herself what a stupid thing to say.

'Yes, rotten bad luck. Only my third week at the front, too. Still, I shall rest up and be able to see my family whilst my wounds mend.'

There was a *toot* from the train and those who'd got off for a walkabout prepared to climb back on.

'I hope it's not a bad wound, sir,' Poppy said, wanting to make a memorable impression on him but not sure how to go about it.

'Well, I'm mashed up a bit, as they say. But apparently there's a wonderful bone-setter in Manchester and I should return to Flanders before too long. I need to get back to my boys. Top notch, they are!'

'Well, I wish you all the best, sir,' Poppy said. Then, before she lost her nerve, she blurted out, 'And do please remember me to your brother!'

Jasper de Vere looked at her, rather surprised, but Poppy just smiled brightly and indicated the nearest carriage. 'Can I help you back on to the train, sir?'

'No, that's quite all right,' he said, hailing a soldier standing by the door. 'My batman will help me. I'm in the officers' carriage.'

Unsure of the etiquette of saying goodbye — was she servant, acquaintance or army nurse? — she finished in a muddle. 'Do kindly excuse me. All the best to you and your family . . . Good wishes and cheerio, sir,' she said and turned to go back on the train.

Unfortunately, one of the injured boys who'd been travelling behind closed blinds had chosen to take a stroll, too, and as Poppy arrived at the train door and reached up to pull herself on board, so did he. Although he had been holding up a cardboard mask to his face, Poppy was close enough to see behind it — and did so before she could stop herself. What she found herself staring at was only a semblance of features: puckered and raw, no hair and hardly a nose, with shrivelled and burned skin around eyes that may have been permanently open. A skull shape, but formed with scorched flesh. A travesty, a ghastly imitation of a face . . .

Poppy recoiled, horrified, gasped for breath. Hauling herself on to the train, she couldn't speak as she pushed past Matthews, gained the safety of the little back kitchen and was violently sick out of the window.

'That's why we keep all new girls out of the way for a little while,' Rees said, after Poppy had apologised profusely, cleaned up after herself and apologised all over again.

'I feel dreadful,' Poppy murmured. 'Poor chap. To have suffered all that and then to have me vomiting at the sight of him.' Tears came into her eyes. 'Do you think I should go and apologise to him? I mean, it's not as if I haven't seen injured people before.' But not quite like that, she thought.

'Apologise? I think not.' Colebrook shook her head. 'Least said and all that. It won't be the first time it happens to him, or the last. I'm afraid the poor lamb will have to learn to live with it.'

'At least you didn't scream,' Matthews said.

'Let's hope he ends up in one of the specialist hospitals,' said Rees. 'They can do wonderful things there.'

Poppy leaned against the wall of the carriage, feeling

depressed beyond words. Fancy her behaving like that! Ma would be really ashamed of her – and Miss Luttrell would be shocked to bits. Did she have no self-control? Did it mean she would never make a proper nurse?

'May I ask you . . . Is it possible for you not to say anything to Sister Malcolm?' she asked the two older VADs in a wobbly voice. 'I think it was because I was feeling a bit funny – I'd just seen an injured soldier who I knew. I'll really try hard never to react like that again.'

'Your secret's safe with us, Pearson,' Rees said.

'We've all done things we were rather ashamed of during our training,' said Colebrook. 'Once I fell asleep during a first-aid lecture – and snored. I almost got chucked out of my unit for that.'

'I'll never forget the time I committed the terrible sin of putting an officer into a ward with twenty Tommies,' said Rees. 'Quite high up he was – a lieutenant colonel, I think. But he was unconscious when he came in and most of his uniform had been blown off, so how was I to know?'

The train continued its steady journey towards Manchester, and Poppy was allowed a ten-minute sit-down to recover herself. She felt strange and unsettled as a result of the encounter with Jasper de Vere, mostly because seeing him had brought his brother to mind so strongly, and of course she was also desperately ashamed of her reaction to the maimed soldier.

*

It was a long, long day. When the train reached Manchester the men were taken by bus, cart or private motor car to the various military hospitals, while Poppy and Matthews cleared away litter, swept through the carriages and left everything as tidy as possible. The train was then loaded up with supplies, clean linens, drugs and other medical requirements for its journey back to Southampton; nothing being allowed on board which might be construed as of a military nature. When she was given a break, Poppy sat down with her notepad.

From a hospital train in Manchester

Dearest Ma,

I have just completed my first assignment as a VAD: a very traumatic train journey from Southampton to Manchester. I should really cross out that word trau-matic, *for if there was any trauma involved in slicing and buttering hundreds of rolls it was far surpassed by seeing at first-hand what these soldiers have endured. It was the most humbling thing to be allowed to do something as simple as butter bread rolls for these brave boys, who all bore wounds of one sort or another. There were also those whose wounds were not visible, but of the inner sort, and one of the senior VADs said to me that these were perhaps the most badly wounded of all.*

These are serious sentiments, yet the men were not all serious, but fun and amusing. You should have heard them, Ma, there was such an amount of comradeship and larks! Lots of dark humour when they were talking about each other's injuries, but each anxious to see that whoever he was with should get served before him. It struck me, listening to them, that war is a very terrible thing, but can bring out the best in people.

And what do you think? On the journey up to Manchester I came across the older de Vere boy, who looks to have a bad leg injury but is 'walking wounded'. He told me that he had only been at the front for three weeks before he was brought down. I expect his mother will be happy to have him back in England again, even if it is only temporary.

This is a selfish thing to say, but I am rather hoping that Billy's regiment doesn't get sent abroad.

Do look after yourself, Ma, and best love to you, Mary and Jane.

From your loving daughter,

Poppy

Chapter Ten

Pte William Pearson,
8903 D Company

Dear Sis,

Well this is a turn-up for the books we are both doing war work. It is different for you of course as i am going to be actually facing the enemy and believe me i have been practising with my bayonet like no ones buisness. When our sergent major says Run Run! and let Fritz have it i make sure that that sack of straw doesnot get up again! When we are not doing bayonet practice we are running across fields with our packs on and doing press-ups and the like. It is important to be fit our sergent major says.

My mates are a solid good crew there are ten of us in the squad and we have promised to lookout for each other and if one of us gets it then whoever has seen what *happened will write to that matey's family and tell them about it.*

We have more or less finished our training now and are waiting to see where we are going to be posted. I saw Ronny Bassett from home last week he is a gunner in the artillery and his regiment have already seen active service in France – lucky blighter! We lads were talking the other night about the war and how ratted off we would be if we dont get a chance to fight. Some units just stay in Blighty the whole time and the nearest they get to fighting is beating up each other. I tell you i will be gutted if i don't get a chance to fight. i want to kill every Fritz I can and earn myself at least one medal and i don't want it for cleaning the majors shoes neither.

Can you write to me Poppy and i will reply as there is not much to do here in the evening all the lads do is write to there sweethearts. I would like to have a girl by the time i go off to fight the war but the trouble is trying to meet someone in a town full of soldiers!!!
i will write to Ma now.

with love from your brother (Private) William Pearson.

Poppy folded up the letter from Billy, smiling and thinking that he must really be bored if he was writing letters. Nonetheless he sounded as if he was actually enjoying himself – fancy him talking about winning medals! She had wondered if he'd be able to submit to army discipline, but she'd obviously underestimated him.

Although nearly a month had gone by since she'd been on the Manchester train, the face of the badly injured soldier was still etched on Poppy's brain. She'd talked to Matthews about it and between them they'd come up with a technique they thought might help. On coming face to face with someone badly injured, they planned to squint their eyes a very small, unnoticeable amount, so that the other, injured features were seen as slightly fuzzy and out of focus. They would then bring it into focus gradually, so that the shock of seeing something awful wasn't too great.

They'd practised on each other and found that it worked quite well – although, of course, they hadn't yet tried it out on a real injured man. Poppy had told Jameson what they were going to do, thinking such a technique might help her, too, but Jameson had just looked at her as though she was mad. 'Everyone will think that VADs are cross-eyed!' she'd said.

That evening, Poppy took Billy's letter into the YWCA canteen, intending to stay there after she'd had supper and reply to him. She usually took her off-duty meals with Matthews – sometimes they even went out for a bite to eat – but that day happened to be Matthews' day off and she'd gone home to see her family.

Poppy fetched some soup and bread, sat down at a table and was joined almost immediately by Jameson carrying her supper tray. Putting the tray down, she pulled a newspaper from her bag.

'I know it's a frightful thing to do, but I feel this compulsion to look through the list of officer casualties to make sure that no one I know is on it,' she said, opening the paper. 'Do you know, so many are being killed that some weeks they have to print a special supplement.'

She began running her finger down the names, murmuring under her breath. Reaching O she gave a little gasp of horror. 'Oh my! I danced with Henry Orlap at my coming-out ball!' she said. 'Such a nice chap, tall and dark with eyes like boot buttons. He made some joke about my ball gown being pink.'

'Why, what's wrong with pink?' Poppy asked.

'Nothing, but my dress wasn't pink,' Jameson said. She frowned slightly, as if surprised by Poppy's ignorance. 'You *must* wear white at Queen Charlotte's Ball. No one would dream of wearing another colour.'

'Oh,' Poppy said. 'Does it say what happened to him?'

'It just says he was killed in enemy action.' She looked behind them to see who was around. 'My father says that more of our boys are dying than the newspapers are reporting,' she whispered to Poppy. 'Probably twice as many.'

'But –'

'It's because it would be bad for morale,' said Jameson. 'Everything's got to be positive – it's always got to look as if we're winning.'

Poppy looked at her, shaking her head and wondering if that could possibly be true. She wondered if Freddie or her brother had yet been posted overseas. A whole regiment could be moved overnight, or so she'd heard. Were these two boys even now in France or Belgium? If either was seriously wounded, how would she know? Sighing, she added salt and pepper and stirred her soup, which unfortunately tasted of its main ingredient, vegetable peelings. All the most nutritious foodstuffs were going to feed the troops.

The war now dominated everything; it was all anyone ever talked about. People speculated how long it would last, how many would be dead by the end of it and what it was costing the nation. They told each other exactly what Kitchener and Asquith were doing wrong, talked about how good things had been before the war, asked where the street entertainers had gone, complained that they couldn't buy half the things on their shopping lists and said that the bread wasn't of the same quality. The war was always to blame.

'*Died in Action . . .*' Jameson murmured, then, finishing this section, moved on to the *Died of Injuries Received* section and went through the *A*s, *B*s and Cs while Poppy was still stirring her soup. Reaching the *D*s, she began, '*Davidson, Dawson, Derekshaw, de Vere, Dillon . . .*'

Poppy went cold. 'Stop!' she cried. 'What did you say?'

Jameson's finger stopped moving downward. 'Dillon. Do you know anyone called Dillon?'

Poppy stared at her. 'The one before that.'

'De Vere?'

Poppy nodded. 'What . . . what was his first name?' she stammered, her lips hardly seeming able to form the words.

'I'll read the whole thing,' Jameson said obligingly. '*De Vere. Second Lieutenant Jasper de Vere* . . .' Poppy, hearing Freddie's brother's name, felt herself go limp with relief – so much so that she sagged against Jameson, who looked at her in surprise before continuing, '. . . *aged 22, who was badly injured during a skirmish at the front, has tragically died of the injuries he received. His funeral will be private, but his sorrowing family are holding a memorial service for him at three o'clock on 1ˢᵗ September in the family chapel on their estate in Mayfield.*' Jameson looked at Poppy with great interest. 'You know the de Veres, do you?'

Poppy closed her eyes and breathed deeply, more relieved than she felt she had any right to be. 'I used to work for them.'

'Oh?'

'I was their parlourmaid,' she added.

'Oh, so you were.'

Poppy did not elaborate. There were worse jobs, she knew, than being a parlourmaid. And at least, unlike Jameson, she knew that stairs should be done from top to bottom and not the other way round, that an egg shouldn't be boiled for forty-five minutes until the water evaporated, and that milk went off if left in the sun – all of which misdemeanours Jameson had been guilty of since she'd arrived. Jameson, though, was a bit like

Freddie de Vere, Poppy had decided. They'd both been spoilt and had had everything done for them. If you were well-to-do, that was just what happened.

'I spoke to him on the train,' Poppy said bleakly. 'His injuries didn't seem too bad. I thought he was all right . . .'

'Will you go to the memorial service?' Jameson asked.

Poppy thought for a moment. She would be able to pay her respects to the family, perhaps tell them the little story about seeing Jasper on the hospital train and, yes, see Freddie again.

'I will if I can get the day off.' She hesitated, then realised that if anyone knew the answer to this question of etiquette, it was Jameson. 'Would it be all right for me to go, do you think?'

'I think that would be fine,' Jameson said. 'Servants are regarded almost as part of the family these days, aren't they?'

'Are they?' Poppy said. She had no idea how Mr and Mrs de Vere regarded her, but she didn't think it was as *family*.

'Anyway, you're not a servant any longer,' Jameson went on, 'and anyone can pay their respects. There are no rights and wrongs about it.'

'Then I'll go,' Poppy decided. 'I'll definitely go.'

The circumstances were certainly not what she'd hoped for, but they meant that she was more than likely to see Freddie again.

Chapter Eleven

Poppy was granted a day's leave to attend the memorial service. She consulted a train timetable and worked out her timings carefully, thinking she would go to visit her mother afterwards, but a few days before received a note from her saying that she and the girls were going to Wales to care for an elderly aunt who'd just had a serious operation.

A pressing concern had been about what she should wear, for she didn't have a black coat or hat with a veil. On asking the advice of Sister Malcolm, however, she was told that her outdoor uniform would be most suitable for a memorial service.

On the day itself, Poppy felt very anxious. She told herself that she must be sensible, that there was a chance Freddie had already been posted overseas and wasn't going to be there for his brother's memorial service — and if that was the case then perhaps it would be a jolly good thing and stop her making a fool of herself. But oh, if he wasn't there, how bereft she'd feel! Or, worse, suppose he was there and simply ignored her?

Before she left that morning, Matthews gave her the once-over. 'You look grand,' she said. 'Just a little too clean and shiny, perhaps.'

'Isn't that good?'

Matthews shook her head. 'No,' she said, 'because it shows that you haven't actually done any nursing. You should look dishevelled and war weary, as if you've just come back from saving lives at the front and have been wearing the same apron for days on end.'

Poppy smiled. 'I thought of boiling it to make the red cross look a bit faded. That's what some of the girls do.'

'Too late for that now,' said Matthews. She looked at Poppy, head on one side. 'It strikes me that you're rather over-concerned about your appearance today. I'm beginning to wonder if there isn't a young man involved. Someone special . . .'

'Well . . .'

'I thought so!'

'But no one knows about it,' said Poppy anxiously. 'And really, nothing's happened between us: only a couple of looks and, well . . .' She looked at her friend wistfully. 'But he did say he'd write to me . . .'

Matthews raised her eyebrows. 'Is he a member of the family you used to work for?'

Poppy nodded.

'Oh Lor',' said Matthews. 'I see trouble ahead.'

'Not at all,' Poppy said. 'I'll probably just look at him, realise how silly I'm being and pull myself together.' But she felt herself blushing . . . she knew she wasn't likely to do any such thing.

Feeling splendidly self-conscious in her outdoor uniform, Poppy walked to the station and caught the train into Waterloo, then took a slow horse bus across to Euston. She didn't want to go on the underground train in case she got smuts all over her face, and there were hardly any of the faster motor buses around; like so much else, they'd gone to do their bit at the front.

The war was everywhere. She passed town halls which had been turned into army recruitment centres and shops which were collection points for second-hand pyjamas for convalescing Tommies. She saw a market stall which was asking for old gramophones, records and mouth organs for the boys in khaki. In fact, everywhere she looked people were doing something; churches were even holding Blanket Days to encourage people to give a warm blanket ready for the coming winter months at the front.

She found London more subdued than it had been just a few months before. People still called out cheery greetings to anyone wearing uniform and applauded passing soldiers, but there was a certain reservation in the air; people were not so gung-ho, for by now nearly everyone had a friend, relative or neighbour who had been injured or killed. Despite all the positive stories in the newspapers, the idea was slowly taking root that the impossible might happen: the Allies might not win the war.

To her delight, however, Poppy also found that the courtesies afforded to men in uniform were now extended to her: people called her 'nursey' and beamed at her, she was ushered to the front of the queue in the newsagent's shop, and from Euston went second class to Mayfield for the price of third.

On the train, she opened the weekly paper she'd bought. This had a supplement giving brief details of some of those who'd died the previous week and how they'd died.

Maurice Green, drowned face down in a trench; Arnold Tallis, killed as a result of a sniper's bullet; Percy Jones, shelled whilst carrying an injured comrade to cover; Edward Topper, died after receiving the full force of a grenade during a skirmish at Gallipoli; George Brown, postie, killed whilst delivering mail to the troops; Frank Cotton and John Tiplady, comrades-in-arms, died together as a result of treading on a land mine . . .

Poppy, her eyes stinging with unshed tears, put the paper down. It was one thing to read a report stating that a certain number of men had died, but this particular newspaper personalised them so that one felt one almost knew them. Even worse was the list of names of boys 'Missing in Action', whose families were desperate for information. Were they dead, captured – or, horrendously, still out there, dying slowly on the contested land?

The leaves on the trees outside Mayfield station were beginning to turn an autumnal gold, but the day was fair and Poppy decided to walk across the parkland in order to see if Airey House looked any different. Sixty officers had now taken up residence in its spacious rooms, and as she made her way through the shrubbery, Poppy could see that a dozen or so hospital beds had been wheeled on to the terrace so that their occupants could receive the benefits of the afternoon sun. Slightly worried, therefore, that one of the men might think she was a real nurse and hail her to ask for something, she ducked behind the hedge and kept out of sight as she passed through the grounds.

She reached the little path which led down to the chapel fifteen minutes before the service was due to start. Some mourners had already gathered outside and Poppy recognised several of the ladies from the Mayfield Comforts Group. There were also two nurses, a small group of army officers and some women from the village, all speaking together in low voices.

After a moment she saw, through the trees, the family's two large black motor cars coming through the iron gates. A man in a black frock coat took his place in front of the first one and, as if at a funeral, walked ahead of the vehicles as they travelled slowly towards the chapel.

She had to get inside before they did! Increasing her pace, Poppy went down the path into the chapel and took a space at the back behind a marble pillar. As the organ began playing, she did some deep breathing to try and gather herself. Please let him be here, she thought, and then chastised herself for thinking of Freddie instead of praying for the soul of his dead brother.

The chapel began to fill up. Two women and a child joined her in the pew, and Poppy became aware of the admiring glances of the little girl.

After a moment she whispered, 'Are you a real nurse?'

Poppy nodded. Well, she was nearly.

The child gave a gasp of awe and her hand reached out to stroke the material of Poppy's coat. 'Have you been in the war?'

Poppy shook her head. 'Not yet.'

'Your coat has lovely gold buttons . . .'

'Yes, it has, hasn't it?'

'I'm going to be a nurse when I grow up.'

'So you can have a coat with gold buttons?' Poppy asked, smiling, and then realised that the organ music had changed to something more sombre and that Freddie de Vere, his elder sister holding on to his arm, had come into the chapel and was looking directly at her. Her smile vanished in an instant, but it was too late – he'd seen her at his brother's memorial service, *smiling*.

Poppy's embarrassment at her blunder lasted all through the service, which took more than an hour. Lots of people spoke about Jasper: the nanny who the de Vere children had had since birth, Jasper's schoolmates, far-flung members of his family and several of his tutors. His commanding officer also gave a speech saying that Jasper had saved the lives of two of his men by going out to rescue them under fire.

'Second Lieutenant de Vere displayed great bravery in going back for a third man, but he was hit by a grenade. He was knocked unconscious into a disused trench and lay hidden from his patrol for a day and a night,' the officer said. 'He was found and received treatment for a severe leg injury, but, tragically, gangrene had set in and it proved impossible to save him.' He shook his head sadly. 'Greater love hath no man than this, that a man lay down his life for his friends.'

A strangled sob came from Mrs de Vere, making Poppy's eyes fill with tears. When Freddie, his voice thick with emotion, rose to give a eulogy about his brother, Poppy lowered her head and found it impossible to look anywhere near where he was standing. How terrible this war was! And she'd actually sent Freddie a white feather to encourage him to join up. Suppose the feather which had shamed him into joining the army ultimately killed him – how would she feel then?

At this time, a year into the war, and with so many men dying, the fashion for extravagant funeral rites and services had passed. There was only one concession to a funeral tea: mourners were invited to take a glass of sherry in the chapel vestry afterwards.

As the service concluded, many of the women began to file out, for the free and easy way that men and women now mixed in London was not yet the way people behaved in the suburbs. Poppy decided that she would go into the vestry, however, for if she didn't take the opportunity to speak to Freddie, she knew she'd regret it. She needed to find out if what she'd seen in Freddie's eyes many months earlier – what she *thought* she'd seen – was real or had been just in her imagination. Even if she made a fool of herself, even if her heart got broken, at least she'd know the truth.

Waiting at the end of the pew to turn left into the vestry instead of going right with those leaving the chapel, Poppy suddenly felt a hand grasping hers.

'You're here!' Molly said, emerging out of the crowd. 'I wondered if you would be.'

Poppy squeezed her friend's hand, delighted to see her.

'But don't you look grand!' Molly said, standing back and gazing at Poppy admiringly. 'Quite the Florence Nightingale.'

'I might look the part, but if anyone here had an accident I'd be quite useless,' Poppy said. 'But you!' She put out a hand and touched Molly's hair, which was frizzy and quite orange in the front. 'You've changed your hair colour!'

'Oh, it's from the chemicals at work,' Molly said. 'It happens to all of us, no matter how much we try to cover it up.'

110

'I quite like it. You look like Mary Pickford.'

Molly giggled. 'We don't even bother with headscarves now. Our supervisor said we should be proud of our orange hair and wear it like a badge.'

'War work!' the two girls said at the same time, and smiled at each other.

'Oh, do come into the vestry with me,' Poppy pleaded.

Molly raised her eyebrows. 'You want to go in there, with the toffs?'

'We have every right. We knew Mr Jasper. Why shouldn't we raise a glass to his memory?'

'Well, I don't know,' Molly said doubtfully. She looked across the chapel. 'Hardly any of the women are going in.'

Poppy stepped down into the aisle and tucked her arm into Molly's. 'We're not like them,' she said. Then she added in a whisper, 'We are *modern* young women, Molly. We're even going to have the vote when the war is over!'

'Blimey,' said Molly.

Poppy saw Miss Philippa Cardew, with her glossy hair and her deep purple velvet coat, as soon as she entered the vestry. So she was still around! Was she here as Freddie's intended, or just as a friend of the family? And where *was* Freddie, anyway? Wasn't he going to look for her? Had he seen her smiling so inappropriately and was cross with her?

Poppy and Molly took a glass of sherry each and made raised-eyebrow faces at each other at their sophistication. After a few moments, Molly became engaged in conversation with a good-looking young officer in full Highland uniform, and Poppy decided she should leave them to it. She made her way towards Mrs de Vere to pay her condolences. As she did so, she was struck with how much more self-assured, how much more womanly she felt dressed as a nurse. She might not be qualified yet, but anyone seeing her wouldn't know it.

She swallowed the last of the sherry and put the empty glass on a passing tray.

'Good afternoon, Mrs de Vere,' she began, reaching her former employer and managing to resist dropping a curtsey to her.

'Poppy? Is it really you?' Mrs de Vere asked in a low voice, peering through her veil.

'It is, madam.'

'How are you, dear? You're a nurse, I see. That's a wonderful vocation . . . There's nothing more important than the welfare of our boys.'

'That's very true,' Poppy said, nodding.

'And I understand that you saw my own dear boy on his way home?'

'I did.' He must have told his family about their meeting, Poppy realised. 'And please do accept my . . . my sincere . . .' And then her voice caught in her throat and she had to stop.

'But do tell me about how he was looking and what he said to you.'

Poppy swallowed. 'Well, he said he'd only had a few weeks at the front, but he hoped he'd be returning there soon because his men were first rate. He seemed in good spirits. I don't believe he had any idea how . . . how poorly he really was, madam.'

'He would have been hiding it, you see,' said Mrs de Vere. 'He was always the bravest of boys as a child. If he fell over and skinned his knee, he'd never cry.'

'He said he was very much looking forward to seeing his family.'

'Did he?' Mrs de Vere was now looking at her with expectant, hopeful eyes.

'And especially to seeing you, ma'am,' Poppy continued, somehow knowing that this was what the other woman wanted to hear. 'He said he couldn't wait to see his dear mother again.'

Mrs de Vere's eyes filled with tears, and she smiled and pressed Poppy's hand wordlessly, gratefully, before she moved on to speak to the next person in line.

Freddie was still nowhere to be seen and Poppy, not wanting to leave, spoke for some time to an elderly gentleman by shouting through his ear trumpet. Ten minutes later, with many of the congregation having left, Molly came up and whispered that her new friend was going to walk her back into town, and she hoped she'd see Poppy soon.

To occupy herself, Poppy moved slowly around the chapel, reading the marble plaques embedded in the wall which commemorated the brave, the industrious and the charitable de Vere dead. By the time she'd gone through them all twice, though, the vestry held no

113

more than a handful of people – and none of them was Freddie de Vere. She would have to leave or it would look very odd indeed. Anyway, she had two trains to catch and had to be back in the hostel by nine o'clock at the latest.

She sighed. Apart from the look when he'd entered the chapel, she hadn't had the smallest amount of contact with Freddie. Was that, then, the end of it all? Surely she'd meant something to him? Surely his feelings had gone a little deeper? She left the chapel, walked down the path towards the road and was just going through the lychgate when she heard footsteps hurrying down the gravel path after her.

'Poppy!' a voice called. 'Please wait!'

Poppy turned. It was him.

He reached her, took her fingers and pressed them between his hands, regarding her with such tenderness that she was struck dumb and could only stare back at him.

'I'm so sorry, Poppy. I nearly missed you,' he said. 'I was at my brother's graveside saying my own goodbyes.' On her not replying, he added, 'He's buried in the crocus lawn at the back of the chapel, you see.'

'You . . . your family must be heartbroken,' Poppy said.

He nodded. 'Mother is especially cut up. Her first-born son and all that.'

Poppy took a deep breath. 'I'm sorry if I looked as if . . .' she began, and was about to continue with an expression of regret for smiling in the church. However, Freddie squeezed her fingers and this tiny gesture effectively stopped her speaking again. So much for the competent and sensible nurse, she thought later; the sophisticated modern miss about to get the vote.

He kept hold of her hand, stood back and gave her an appraising look. 'You make a splendid nurse, Poppy.'

'I feel a little bit of a fraud,' she confessed. 'I haven't done any real nursing yet.'

'Well, you certainly look the part.' He hesitated. 'I must apologise,' he said then. 'I said I'd write to you, but I haven't. The thing is, I find it quite difficult to write a decent letter. At school we were taught how to write essays and do translations and so on, but not how to write letters. At least, not *that* sort of letter.'

'Which sort?'

'Well, you know . . .'

'Do I?' Poppy said, blushing a little.

'We don't get taught how to write letters to young ladies.'

'Oh. I see,' Poppy said, her heart beating fast.

He shook his head. 'I've often thought of our meeting in London and cursed my stupidity. I should have helped Aunt Maud in with her trunk and then come to find you. What a chump you must have thought me!'

'I did not at all!'

'And then later at the house I tried to speak to you, but you always seemed to be with Cook or Molly or someone, and I didn't know what to say anyway.' He gazed at her. 'No more than I do now. Believe me, this sort of thing is all very new to me.'

'I need to get to the station,' she said, her heart thudding at her own forwardness. 'Perhaps we could walk down and talk on the way.'

But Freddie was shaking his head. 'I'm so sorry, Poppy,' he said. 'The cars are taking all the family back to London and Mother has a meal booked at a hotel somewhere. But I *will* write to you. Next week, I promise.'

'That would be lovely.' A letter from Freddie, she thought, would be almost as good as speaking to him. In a letter, he must surely talk about his feelings.

She gave him her YWCA address and he wrote it down carefully in a small leather notebook.

'If my regiment gets deployed abroad we'll be going through Southampton,' he said, putting the book away. 'If there's time, we can meet and do something nice – go dancing, perhaps?'

'Oh, how lovely!' Poppy felt breathless at the very thought of it. One moment she'd been tragically unloved, the next she was being whirled around a ballroom in Freddie's arms.

'I must go,' Freddie said ruefully, and he glanced back towards the chapel, where the lone figure of Mrs de Vere could be seen, outlined against the late sun. 'Mother's looking for me. Goodbye . . . Farewell . . . I'm sure we'll see each other soon.'

There was a tiny moment when they both stared at each other, unsure of what to do next, then his lips came down upon hers in a butterfly's touch of a kiss, quick and tender.

'Goodbye,' he said. 'Take very good care of yourself.'

'And he told me that his regiment hoped to be going to France soon and on their way to the ship he would see me and take me dancing!' Poppy said the next morning, finishing telling the tale to Matthews and Jameson but leaving out the kiss until she and Matthews were on their own. She helped herself to another portion of corn-flakes; she'd be working from eight in the morning until eight at night and knew she'd never last otherwise.

'You won't be allowed to go dancing,' Jameson said immediately. 'It's in the agreement we signed when we joined. No consorting with members of the opposite sex, and certainly no dancing.'

'Oh, that'll be all right,' Matthews said. 'You'll just have to say he's your brother and you're seeing him before he goes to France. My sister has had quite a few different brothers pass through Dover at various times! You still won't be given permission to go dancing – even with a brother – but no one will know. After all, they can't expect us to live like nuns.'

'Actually, I think they do,' said Jameson. 'But you say this is a de Vere boy?'

Poppy nodded. '*The* de Vere boy. There's only one now.'

Jameson looked at her doubtfully. 'And does his mother know about you?'

Poppy shrugged. She really didn't want to think about *that*. She wanted to think about the two of them being most romantically, wonderfully in love – for they were, surely? She wanted to think about Freddie going off to fight and distinguishing himself in some way, and of herself working alongside him, a talented and dedicated nurse.

Just let him come to Southampton soon!

The letter was delivered the following morning. It was in a parchment envelope that proved to be tissue-lined. Addressed in dark blue ink, it had neat writing and bore the de Vere insignia on the back.

Poppy knew instinctively that it wasn't from Freddie. She also knew before she opened it that she wasn't going to like its contents.

The embossed address at the top, *Airey House, Mayfield*, had been crossed through.

Somerset

September 1915

Miss Pearson,
I write to say how shocked I was by your behaviour at my elder son's memorial service. I clearly saw what was going on and believe you must have come with the express intention of making a play for Frederick, acting as you did in the most brazen manner.

Frederick is now our only son and, of course, the de Vere heir, so one expects to come across young women fortune-hunters, but to attempt to ensnare him at such a time, when he is attempting to deal with the sudden and cruel death of his brother, seems very low behaviour indeed.

I will have no hesitation about informing both Devonshire House and your family of your conduct unless you cease all communication with my son forthwith.

Mrs V. de Vere

Poppy, furious and indignant, showed the letter to Matthews, who gave her a reassuring hug.

'There's absolutely nothing she can do. All right, she says she'll inform your family, but really – so what? Anyway, your mother's gone away, hasn't she?'

Poppy nodded. 'She's staying in Wales.'

'So . . . Mrs High and Mighty: what on earth did you do to make her so angry?'

Poppy sighed. 'We kissed . . .'

'You didn't tell me that before!' Matthews said, pretending shock but unable to prevent a smile showing through.

'Just the smallest kiss . . . oh! We were standing at the bottom of the slope and she was standing at the top. She must have seen us.'

'She had no business looking!'

'No, I know . . . but I shouldn't like her to tell the matrons at Devonshire House about it.'

'What could she possibly say?' Matthews said, spreading margarine across her toast. 'It's a free country. Anyone is allowed to fall in love with anyone else.'

'Are you sure?'

'Yes, and it's going to happen more and more,' said Matthews airily. 'A few years back a boy might have given a girl the glad eye but never bothered to take it further. Now, with everyone being separated and a generation of men going off to war and getting killed, there's an urgency about falling in love. Everyone wants to live life to the full.'

'So what should I do? Write back to her?'

'Certainly not,' Matthews said. 'Just wait until Freddie comes to Southampton and then go dancing with him and have the most splendid time.'

'Yes . . .' said Poppy doubtfully.

'And sometime during the evening you could mention that his mother doesn't seem too happy about you seeing each other. I bet he'll say that it's none of her rotten business and that'll be the end of it. Being forbidden to see you will only make him keener.'

'Do you really think so?'

'I really do,' Matthews assured her.

Chapter Twelve

The following morning, Sister Malcolm arrived at the hostel at first light with a wad of paperwork under her arm, ready to tell the new VADs which hospital they'd be assigned to. They had all gained their certificates in first aid and home nursing, so knew how to pack and bandage wounds (at least, simulated ones), to bed-bath a patient as modestly as possible, to sterilise bandages, apply poultices, take temperatures and to be discreet in the giving out and collection of bed pans. Which of these duties they would be permitted to do, however, would be entirely down to the ward sister they would be working under.

There were just ten of them now. Two of their number, having come from homes where a multitude of servants had seen to their every need, had found the long hours and sometimes tedious tasks too much for them. Poppy, by contrast, hadn't found the hours as long or the tasks as tiring as when she was working for the de Veres.

Experience in service, she thought, was an ideal starting point for a girl who wanted to be a VAD.

The girls gathered in the YWCA common room, all nervous but rather excited at the thought of getting their hands on real patients.

'There are scores of hospitals within the Southampton area,' Sister Malcolm began, 'but the Royal Victoria Military Hospital at Netley is, without doubt, the largest of these, and its capacity has recently been vastly increased by the addition of a hut hospital in the surrounding grounds. Each of these huts contains at least two fully trained nurses, but they also rely very much on Red Cross VADs to carry out the day-to-day work. As the war continues and the number of injured men increases, they will be in need of more of you. You will therefore *all* be going to Netley.'

Poppy and Matthews exchanged glances. They'd both been hoping that they would be taken on by a small hospital, thinking it would be easier to get to know the patients that way and to gain a position of responsibility. A very large establishment was not what they'd wanted.

'How big is it, Sister?' someone asked.

'Nearly two hundred new huts have been built,' Sister Malcolm replied.

'But . . . *huts*,' said Jameson in a rather disparaging tone.

Sister Malcolm looked at her. 'Did you think you'd be working in the Ritz Hotel, Jameson?'

'Well, no, but –'

'The huts are *wards*. They are bang up to date, they have their own kitchens, bathrooms and nursing stations and all the equipment you'd expect to find in a brand new hospital.'

Jameson nodded, contrite, but Sister hadn't finished with her.

'I'm sorry we can't put you in a brick-built place, Jameson, but there hasn't been time to construct one – not when more and more men with the most dreadful injuries are coming in every day. Every single day!'

Jameson looked uncomfortable. 'No. I see that. Sorry, Sister,' she murmured.

'Excuse me, Sister,' Poppy asked, trying to help out Jameson. 'How many beds are there in the hospital altogether?'

Sister Malcolm consulted her paperwork. 'Before the new wards were built, Netley could hold a thousand men. Now it can house nearly two and a half thousand. They deal with surgical cases, medical cases, men with dysentery, TB and nerve trouble. In fact, they take on every type of war-related illness and surgery.'

Poppy gasped. There had been perhaps three or four hundred soldiers on the train going to Manchester, and it had been shocking to see so many and with such critical injuries. But to realise that there was a hospital in this local area with a total of two and a half thousand beds just for war injuries! It was a figure almost beyond her imagination.

'Are you shocked by that number of casualties?' Sister Malcolm asked quietly.

Poppy nodded, as did some of the others.

'I'm afraid every encounter, every battle, now produces hundreds, sometimes thousands, of casualties.'

The girls were silent, trying to take in the magnitude of what faced them.

Sister Malcolm shook her head slowly. 'It's enough to break one's heart. Many of the young lads whom Kitchener recruited at the start of the war didn't survive their first battle. We're losing a whole generation of young men.'

'But the Germans are losing young men, too, aren't they?' said one of the girls.

Sister Malcolm looked at her. 'Do you think that makes it any better? Any fairer?' she asked, and the girl reddened. 'A whole generation wiped out in Germany, in France, Belgium and England. Where's the sense in that?' Finishing the sentence with a catch in her voice, Sister Malcolm then stared out of the window for a full two minutes. When she turned back to the girls, she said, 'I realise I have a rather unorthodox view of war, one that the majors and generals might not agree with. I'm just relieved not to be a man, for then I'd be forced to fight and I don't know if I could.' She hesitated, as if she was trying to keep her feelings under control, then added, 'I just want to emphasise that at Netley you will have an enormous number of young men to care for, all of them grievously wounded.'

Poppy closed her eyes for a moment and visualised a long, long line of hospital beds, each bearing an injured soldier, stretching off into the hazy distance.

'Once you begin nursing there must be no slacking, no laziness, no grumbling about following orders,' said

Sister Malcolm. 'The men who are dependent on us have all suffered on our behalf. We mustn't let them down.'

After some more details about afternoons off and annual leave, the girls put on their outer coats and walked down to the station in crocodile formation, two by two.

'Like good little girls on a school trip,' Poppy said to Matthews.

'But we're not. We're real VADs!' said Matthews.

On their way to the station they drew many looks and some applause. Holding their heads high, swishing their skirts, they tried not to look too pleased about it.

Jameson, who was walking directly behind them, said in a loud whisper, 'Do you know what the Tommies call us VADs?'

'No. Do tell!' said Poppy.

'Very Adorable Darlings,' Jameson whispered.

Poppy and Matthews laughed.

'I do hope some good-looking chap falls madly in love with me,' Matthews said. 'A captain, ideally.'

The military hospital at Netley was Britain's principal reception hospital for the huge numbers of war casualties arriving from France, and a branch of the railway had been constructed to convey troops directly from ship to hospital. This way, the injured men only had to limp, stagger or be stretchered a few final feet from the train into bed.

Netley was an attractive building but far too large to be practical, consisting of 138 wards and stretching a full quarter-mile. VADs running errands for ward sisters found themselves covering miles over a day. The girls, used to the small cottage hospitals, were amazed to see it.

'Look at the size of it! We'll get in there and never find our way out again,' Poppy said as they approached the mighty building.

'We'll have to tie the end of a piece of string to the door handle and unroll it as we go,' Matthews replied.

'I don't think that would be a very good idea – people could trip up,' Jameson said seriously, and Poppy and Matthews stifled giggles.

When the girls were allocated their wards, Poppy found that she was to be working under a fully qualified nurse, Sister Kay, in Hut 59, a surgical ward mostly holding ordinary servicemen who had lost one or more of their limbs as well as having supplementary injuries. Matthews was based on a convalescent ward, and Jameson, who spoke German, was told she would be looking after German prisoners of war who needed hospital treatment. She was rather indignant at this, for, as she complained to Sister Malcolm, she'd volunteered specifically to nurse British officers.

'Perhaps you have,' Sister said, 'but if your brother was badly injured and taken prisoner by the German army, wouldn't you like to know that he was being tended by someone who spoke his language?'

The new VADs were taken on a tour of the main hospital building so they could start to learn where the various kitchens, operating theatres, storerooms, linen rooms, training areas and chapels were located.

Afterwards, Poppy made her way to Hut 59, which was a sturdy wooden hut in a huge open field containing over two hundred similar huts.

She hung up her coat and hat in the annexe, feeling scared of what might be expected of her. It fell as if she was about to act in a starring role at the theatre, but hadn't yet learned her lines.

She edged into the ward and stared about her. This was *her* ward, she thought, and these were the boys *she* was going to look after. It was a long room with a row of beds running down each side of it, each with a dark wool blanket tucked in tightly, a blue counterpane with its top folded down and a linen sheet as white and crisp as an envelope over that. Most of the beds had occupants; a few were empty. Right down the middle of the room was a long dining table bearing pots of ferns, and this was flanked by dining chairs. Pinned all over the walls were maps, framed photographs of the King and Queen, cartoons, sheet music and some articles cut out of newspapers. *Let them have it!* Poppy read. *Not long now, boys!* and *The little women at home!*

She stood unseen for a moment, feeling shy and awkward, then went towards the sister in charge, who was sitting at a desk at the top of the ward.

Sister Kay was middle-aged, gaunt, with long grey hair which was braided around her head in an old-fashioned style. She also, to Poppy's eyes, looked stern and rather terrifying.

'Sister Kay?'

The sister sighed. 'I suppose you must be the new VAD.'

Poppy nodded. 'Poppy Pearson.'

'I can only hope that you turn out to be more capable than the last one.'

Poppy didn't answer this, having no knowledge of who this might have been.

Sister Kay looked Poppy up and down carefully, checked that her skirts didn't show a glimpse of ankle and that the Red Cross band was on the proper arm, then introduced her to Nurse Gallagher, an attractive and experienced nurse in her thirties, who, it turned out, had been working at Netley since before the war. Also on Ward 59 for part of the time was Smithers, a male orderly who was there to do the heavy lifting and carry out some of the men's more intimate tasks, and another VAD who, happily, turned out to be Moffat, whose bath water had been stolen by Jameson. Poppy, who'd come to like Moffat, was immensely reassured to see her there.

'Be prepared to work harder than you've ever worked before,' Moffat said by way of greeting. 'But also be prepared to love every minute of it.'

'I'm not scared of hard work – just of doing something daft.'

'Well, let's get you going,' Moffat said. She looked at her watch. 'You've missed the morning dressings round, but you're just in time for the dinner trays.'

Poppy looked at her blankly.

'Every mealtime – breakfast, dinner and tea – you have to take round the trays laid ready for the boys' meals,' she said. She nodded towards the door. 'Come with me and I'll show you.'

Poppy obediently followed her from the hut into a small kitchen in the annexe. It was lined with shelves and contained a sink and gas ring as well as a few basic items of kitchen equipment, a pile of tin trays, plates, cutlery and condiments.

'There are forty-odd trays to lay up, each with knife, fork and spoon, salt and pepper pots,' said Moffat. 'You give each man a tray first – he'll tell you if he's eating in bed, or at the table – then wait for the soup to arrive. You ladle out eight bowlfuls at a time, put them on the trolley and bring them round. And no larger portions for the ones you like the look of. No favouritism!'

Poppy, rather startled at this, said, 'Favouritism? I've hardly even *seen* any men yet!'

'Ah, they're a lovely bunch,' Moffat said. 'Sweet as sweet can be! They're regular Tommies either waiting for surgery or getting over it. They've had a hard time and are just pleased to be back home tucked up in bed.'

Poppy smiled in sympathy at this.

'Oh, they'll lead you a dance sometimes and you *will* have your favourites, but don't let Sister Kay find out or she'll run you out of here quicker than a rat along a drainpipe. That's what happened to our last VAD.'

'She got run out?'

Moffat nodded. 'She was a flirty little thing, but the boys liked her well enough and she liked them. A little too much, judging by what went on in the linen cupboard.'

'Goodness,' said Poppy, and would have liked to have heard more, but Moffat had gone back to the ward.

Poppy loaded up the trolley with trays and took them out, to be greeted by a chorus of wolf whistles. ('Just as if I'd been a ballet dancer making an entrance!' she told Matthews later.)

'They've just been told that you're our new VAD,' Moffat said to the flustered Poppy. 'Take no notice. They like to make a girl blush.'

There were some more whistles, calls of 'Over here, nurse!' and 'I'm going to need some help with my soup!' In the end Sister Kay stood up and merely *looked* at the boys she perceived to be the main culprits. It was a look that did the trick.

Back in the little kitchen in the annexe, soup and bread had arrived from one of the hospital's main kitchens. Poppy ladled out portions, loaded up the trolley as quickly as she could and wheeled it into the ward.

She kept her head down as she moved along the ward delivering trays to table and bed, partly from shyness and partly – remembering the troop train – in case she saw anything too disturbing. There was one bed which had screens placed right round it and Poppy, who'd been regarding this with some anxiety, was happy to comply with Sister Kay's order not to disturb the man sleeping within.

After the soup, a tray of meat pie, plus pans full of stewed carrots and greens were delivered, and Smithers the orderly helped Poppy distribute them to the men at some speed, so that they wouldn't get cold. After this came stewed apples and custard.

Poppy dashed about, going backwards and forwards from ward to kitchen several times for items she'd forgotten. While all this was going on, Moffat and Smithers cut up the meat for those boys who only had one arm, fed those who had no use of their arms at all, and helped a man lying flat who could only take his nourishment with the aid of a feeding cup.

At the end of the meal, Poppy had a few moments to familiarise herself and look around the ward before she collected the dirty plates. As she did so, she realised that the eyes of everyone there were upon her, as if they were waiting for something.

Suddenly the boy in the bed closest to her flung his one leg out from the covers and, leaning on a chair for balance, sang, '*Say goodbye to Tommy Atkins, He's the chap you're going to miss, Wave a hand to Tommy Atkins . . .*'

'Private Wilson!' Sister Kay's voice boomed down the ward.

'*. . . Though he'd much prefer a kiss!*'

'That's quite enough, thank you,' Sister said. 'This is a hospital ward, not a music hall.'

The singer gave a deep bow in Poppy's direction and, to cheers from his fellow patients, got back into bed. Poppy, scarlet-faced, scurried to the relative safety of the little kitchen and composed herself before taking round mugs of tea.

After the food came the washing-up – seemingly as much as they used to have at Airey House after a party, Poppy thought, although then she'd had Molly and a little girl from the village to help her. Following tea, every boy there had his hot-water bottle refilled for afternoon rest, and following that, the beds were tidied and smoothed ready for visiting time. The visitors were mostly, if the patient came from nearby, the boys' families. However, there was also an occasional fiancée and several 'Good Eggs', as Sister called them – middle-aged ladies who didn't know the boys personally, but, perhaps not having sons of their own, wanted to give them little treats.

It was teatime before Poppy knew it: egg and cress sandwiches, Victoria sponge and more mugs of tea. Then came the reapplication of some bandages, the taking round of bedpans and painkillers ('We've hardly got any drugs – they've all gone to the front,' Moffat confided) and yet more tidying of beds before the night staff came on. Their arrival signalled that Poppy's shift was over. Yawning profusely, she dragged herself home, wondering how on earth the previous 'flirty little thing' had ever had the energy to entertain boys in the linen cupboard.

Back at the hostel, she found a letter propped up on her pillow and, seeing it in the dim light, thought it might be a letter from Freddie. She was deeply disappointed to find that it was from her brother.

Hi Sis,
Just a quick note to say my regiment will be passing through southampton, from the station to the docks to catch a troopship late afternoon on 12ᵗʰ September.

This is not common knowledge and we dont no the name of the ship we are going on but my mate Ron found out because his girl works as a clerk in the war office and always looks to see whose going where. Matey says its good we no, as we can get stocked up with ciggies and so on. I am letting you no too in case you can come down to the docks and wave me of. Youll be right proud and you can tell our ma of it.

We are really looking forward to knocking it to 'em. We have started a contest to see who gets the most jerries the prize is a jug of beer in the Flying Duck at home.
Your brother,

William.

PS I am mostly called William now as someone said that Billy is a kids name.

Poppy read the letter again and then put it away. She would certainly ask Sister Kay if she could go and wave him off, but not yet, for she didn't quite feel up to asking favours. She would see how the next few days in Hut 59 went . . .

Chapter Thirteen

'N urse!'

It was only Poppy's second day at Netley and, not feeling a bit like a nurse, she didn't respond to the call. The previous day had been alarming, a chaotic mixture of tasks performed (not terribly well, she'd thought) one after the other at the command of Sister Kay, with not a break between nor space to draw breath. The caller couldn't want *her*, she thought; as it was quite impossible that she could be mistaken for a real nurse.

'Nurse!' The call came again, more urgently, echoing down one of the corridors of the main hospital.

Poppy turned to see a young man, wearing the buff jacket of an orderly, waving to her.

'Oh, sorry!' she said, going towards him. 'I didn't think you meant me. I'm not really a nurse.'

'You're dressed like one,' he said.

'Well, I'm a nursing VAD, but I've only just started here.' She stared at the young man, who was pale and worried-looking, with beads of sweat breaking out on his forehead. 'Are you all right?'

He shook his head, panting slightly. 'No . . . It's my first day and I was just lifting someone and . . .'

'You've seen something disturbing, haven't you?' Poppy said.

'I don't . . .'

'Do you feel sick? Faint?' Poppy asked swiftly. 'You ought to sit down.' She put her hand under his arm and guided him to a bench, keen to put what she knew about first aid into operation. 'You need to put your head between your legs and –'

'Wait!' The young man struggled to sit up, but Poppy pushed his head down again.

'Just stay like that for a moment. You know, I saw someone disfigured on the troop train and had just the same reaction as you. It's terribly embarrassing but perfectly understandable.'

'No! Nurse, or whoever you are . . .'

'I'm called Pearson,' Poppy said.

He jerked his head up and shrugged off her hand from the back of his neck. 'Well, Pearson, if you'll just give me a moment to explain. I was lifting a man from a stretcher into bed and when I looked round the group I was with had gone. I've been dashing about everywhere trying to find them.'

'The group?' Poppy said uncertainly.

He nodded. 'I'm with Doctor Armstrong's team, training to be a field doctor. I'm going out to help patch up battle wounds.'

'Oh,' Poppy said. 'You're a doctor . . .' She felt herself beginning to turn red.

'Almost,' he said. 'I'm awaiting confirmation.'

'But you're wearing an orderly's jacket,' she said weakly.

'Yes, and you're wearing a nurse's outfit.' He stood up. 'If you must know, I dressed the wound of someone who was bleeding badly and stained my own jacket, so an orderly lent me his spare one. I could hardly go round the place looking like a . . . a . . .'

'An axe murderer?' Poppy finished.

He smiled suddenly, a wide smile that lit up his face. 'I didn't think I looked like an axe murderer, but thank you for that, Pearson. Anyway, as I was saying, I was with a group of student doctors on a tour of the building and got left behind. I've been going up and down corridors looking for them ever since.'

'I'm so sorry,' Poppy said. Doctors and surgeons were regarded as minor gods by everyone from the matron downward, so it was mortifying to think that she'd grabbed hold of one and tried to force his head between his knees. '*Really* sorry,' she repeated.

'Never mind that now.' He sighed. 'Now, Pearson, have you any idea where the haematology lab really is? Everyone I've asked has sent me off in a different direction.'

Poppy nodded. 'I know exactly. I had to go there yesterday and it's very near the hut I've been assigned to.' She pointed. 'Along this way, across the corridor and through the swing doors on the right.'

He set off at a brisk pace. 'I'm much obliged to you, Pearson,' he called over his shoulder.

She glanced after him. A doctor! And quite charming, she thought, with his grey eyes and his wide smile. But the hundred and one demands of the day soon took over her thoughts.

All was strangely quiet in Hut 59 when Poppy went in. She said a cheerful good morning to the other staff and was given a raised-eyebrow sort of look from Moffat. When she went into the annexe to begin preparing the breakfast trays, the other VAD came in after her.

'Just to let you know that we're all a little subdued today – we had a man die in the night,' Moffat said in a low voice. 'Really nice chap. Sister Kay was very fond of him.'

'Oh dear. I'm so sorry,' Poppy said. She hesitated. 'Who was it? The man behind the screen?'

Moffat shook her head. 'No, a nice regular army sergeant who never gave anyone any trouble. He died just when we all thought he was safe. Nothing directly to do with his injury – the doctors think delayed shock led to his having a heart attack.' She sighed. 'When I got here this morning I saw the stretcher being taken out of the ward with a Union Jack covering it.'

Poppy saw tears in the other girl's eyes and felt her own well up in sympathy. 'I'm really sorry,' she said again, feeling inadequate.

'I'm afraid it sometimes happens like that,' Moffat said, sniffing. 'You get a chap in, you patch him up and sort him out, and then he goes and dies. Mind you,' she went on after a moment, 'he was due to have his other leg off today.'

'Oh. So he would have been . . .'

Moffat nodded. 'A double amputee. He was dreading it, although we all kept telling him he'd be fixed up with false legs and be as good as new.'

'*Good as new*,' Poppy repeated dubiously.

'You have to tell them that. His wife visited him here, though she couldn't come that often as she's got three little girls. Now Sister will have to tell her the news and there's nothing worse – not when you think your chap has come through the worst and is safely back in Blighty – than to find out he's dead.'

'No . . .' Poppy breathed. How dreadful . . . she couldn't imagine . . .

Moffat squeezed her hand and they shared a look – a sympathetic, fortifying, we're-all-in-this-together look – then she went back into the ward. Poppy breathed deeply, blew her nose and began to load up a trolley with bowls, jugs of milk and spoons for the boys' breakfasts.

'Sugar, hot water, milk, syrup, salt, butter for toast . . .' she muttered to herself like a mantra. Maybe this morning she'd do better.

While she was still frowning and counting out spoons, Smithers the orderly came in. 'Now, *breakfast*,' he said. 'I came in to tell you that some of the boys' relatives have brought in new-laid eggs for them.'

Poppy nodded. 'Oh yes, I saw the notices asking for eggs to be donated.'

'Some like them soft boiled with bread-and-butter soldiers; some hard boiled; some will only eat them tipped out on to a plate; a couple prefer scrambled.'

Poppy's heart sank. 'Oh, no! Really?'

Smithers raised his eyebrows. 'After all those boys have done for us, don't you think they deserve an egg cooked the way they want it?'

'Oh, of course they do,' Poppy said guiltily. 'I was just wondering how I was going to . . .' She stopped because he was chuckling at her.

'It's all right – I'm having you on,' he said. 'Just boil up a dozen or so eggs – whatever you've got – in a big saucepan and give them all four minutes. First come, first served. Their chums will see to it that those who don't get an egg today will get one tomorrow.'

Poppy set the egg water to boil and then went in with the trolley to serve porridge and cups of tea. The men seemed rather glum and only cheered up when she announced that she couldn't find any egg cups to put the eggs in and she would have to go and borrow a dozen from the next ward. This led to a score of egg-related puns about the previous VAD having hidden them *egg*stra well, it being a *yolk* where they'd gone, and if she could borrow some it would be *egg*sellent. Sister Kay kept a straight face throughout most of this, but when one of the lads said something about not sleeping well and feeling *egg*shausted, even she managed a smile.

Breakfast over, Sister Kay, Nurse Gallagher and Moffat had started the morning dressings round, and Poppy was about to begin tidying the men's lockers when she heard Sister saying something about giving the new VAD some bandaging practice. A moment later Moffat came over and said they were to swap jobs.

Poppy looked at her in alarm.

'You'll be fine,' Moffat said. 'Dressings are changed every day, sometimes twice a day, so it's just as well that you learn the basics.' She must have seen the look of apprehension on Poppy's face because she added, 'Just remember: look the patient in the eye and keep a smile on your face.'

Poppy went to join Sister and Nurse behind the dressings trolley, praying that she would not faint or be sick, but act sensibly, maturely and positively. If faced with a gruesome facial injury, she would act out the plan that she and Matthews had devised.

I'll be fine. I'll be fine, she said to herself, and was awfully glad that no one there knew about the episode on the troop train.

There was a gramophone in the ward, a present from the grateful father of a boy who'd been patched up and sent home, and Smithers wound it up and put on a record of popular music-hall songs.

'They like the songs?' Poppy asked Moffat, as several of the boys started humming, whistling or singing.

'Well, yes. It concentrates their minds while their bandages are being changed, gives them something else to think about.'

Poppy nodded.

'And sometimes stops the poor things screaming,' Moffat added wryly.

For some of the patients, having their dressings changed was painful. For others it was *very* painful. If the wound had bled overnight and the cotton wool and gauze had stuck to the raw place, it was especially bad. Brave though they were, the cleaning and re-bandaging of their wounds caused many young men to weep. Unfortunately for the nervous Poppy, one of the first to be attended to, Private Johnson, had one of the worst wounds of all: not only had his left arm been blown off, but he had a huge hole in his side.

'Walked right into it, caught the explosion just as I turned,' he said to Poppy, as the blood-caked dressings were peeled off him.

Poppy stood by to put the sodden bandages in a bowl, trying to be an automaton, trying not to wince, grimace or run out screaming. If he can stand it, she thought to herself, so can I. *If he can stand it, so can I . . .*

Carefully, Sister Kay and Nurse Gallagher turned Private Johnson on to his good side. He'd been humming *My Love and I* when they'd reached him, but now his face was white and taut with pain.

'Where did you say your home town was, Private Johnson?' Nurse Gallagher asked, sponging the old bandage to soften it and then encourage it to come off.

Private Johnson gritted his teeth and managed to say, 'Richmond.'

'Ah yes. I believe there's a lovely park there.'

Private Johnson gave a groan.

'I believe you said you'd been there, Pearson,' Nurse Gallagher said to Poppy.

'Oh, yes, I have!' Poppy said, realising that she was being asked to pick up the conversational ball. 'Lovely . . . deer and things. And other wildlife.' She thought of all the parks she'd ever visited and what they'd had in them. 'Grass snakes, as well, if you're not careful . . . and wild flowers in spring.'

Private Johnson let out a shuddering breath, then said, 'My wife and I . . . picnics there last summer . . . before the war started.' As Nurse Gallagher released the last piece of dressing, he bit his lip so hard that it drew blood. 'We've got a picnic basket. Wedding present . . . and . . . and . . .' but the pain was too much for him and he fainted.

'Poor chap,' Sister Kay said. 'Let's work quickly now.'

Poppy held the enamel dish steady, looking at Private Johnson's face so that she wouldn't have to look at the ghastly open wound, while Sister and Nurse cleaned and dried it, packed it out with sphagnum moss and re-bandaged it.

'Sit beside him and hold his hand until he comes round,' Sister said. 'Get him a warm drink if he wants one.'

Poppy drew up a stool beside the bed and took Private Johnson's hand, feeling his pulse to make sure it didn't falter. Sister and Nurse moved on, but it was several moments before Private Johnson came round.

'They've finished,' Poppy said as soon as he opened his eyes. 'It's all over.'

'All over for today,' Private Johnson said, pale and faint. 'God knows how many more days I'll have to go through it.'

Poppy squeezed his hand. 'Would you like a warm drink? Some cocoa?'

But he didn't seem to hear her. 'Course, my best mate wasn't as lucky as me,' he said hoarsely. 'On watch, he was, when a sniper got him right in the throat. Severed his windpipe and that was it. Gone in a flash.'

Poppy gave him a sympathetic look. 'Well, *you're* still with us,' she said. 'And with a bit of luck, maybe next summer the war will be over and you'll be picnicking in the park again.'

It was an awfully trite remark, she thought afterwards, but really, what was she supposed to say? And what were the chances of such a hideous wound ever healing? Sister Malcolm had told them that, with the worst wounds, gangrene – often leading to death – was a constant danger, no matter how carefully the men were nursed. Private Johnson's only hope was a skin graft; but it seemed a huge amount of space to cover . . .

Once Private Johnson was sitting up, propped by pillows and grey of face, Poppy rejoined Nurse and Sister. By now they had reached Thomas Stilgoe, who was the only person in the ward called by his first name. He was seventeen, or so he said, but so small and thin he looked no more than twelve. He'd been acting as a messenger taking notes along the trenches from one unit to another, when he'd trodden on a landmine which had blown off most of his leg below the knee. The rest of it had been amputated on the field there and then, with what small amount of painkillers had been available.

'Pearson, this is our special boy,' said Nurse Gallagher, and she set swinging the small stuffed bear that someone had attached to the end rail of his bed.

'Do leave off, Nurse,' Thomas said.

'The men have made a bit of a pet of him,' Nurse Gallagher said to Poppy. She lowered her voice. 'Although he's been very quiet lately. We're taking care that he doesn't go into a depression.'

'Thomas will want his food mashed up!' someone called.

'And his milk in a feeding bottle . . .'

'That's enough!' Sister Kay said to the ward. She began to unwrap the blood-soaked bandage. 'Are you feeling all right, Thomas?'

The boy, now looking very pale, nodded, but bit hard on an edge of the blanket as the stump of the amputated leg was exposed to the air. It looked dreadful, Poppy thought as she concentrated on smiling, like something hanging in a butcher's shop.

'The wound will need to be surgically tidied up soon,' Nurse said to Poppy, 'because it was done in a hurry in a dugout. And the surgeons will want to get out one or two last pieces of shrapnel.'

She and Sister Kay sponged, dabbed and trickled clean water over the livid flesh before tying it up in a neat parcel.

'Bear up, lad,' Sister Kay kept saying to him. 'Nearly over. Bear up . . .'

'Have your people been to see you yet?' Poppy asked when the job had been completed and Thomas was lying limp and exhausted from the effort of 'bearing up'.

'There's only me ma and she's away in Newcastle,' Thomas said. 'She can't get down because of the bairns.'

'It *is* a long way for her to come,' said Sister Kay sympathetically, 'but we'll see what we can do.'

They moved on to the next patients, with Poppy going backwards and forwards carrying away used dressings, fouled water and bloodied pyjamas, and passing Sister clean bandages, boiled water and – if she could find them – clean tops and trousers. As she worked she tried to familiarise herself with the different injuries which the men had endured, learning a little about each man. Private Franklin had had both arms blown off when he attempted to chuck out a grenade which had been thrown into his trench; Private Freeman had lost his left arm and most of his shoulder in a mortar attack; Sergeant Carter lost a footful of toes through stepping on a shell; Private Miller's arm and right side were slit open by a bayonet and it wasn't clear what internal injuries he had; Private Jones had lost an arm and was full of shrapnel; Private Brownley had lost an arm and an ear, and couldn't remember how. Some had already had surgery; some were waiting for it. One or two had picked up infections on the battlefield and needed to be carefully nursed through pneumonia, typhoid or septicaemia before they could start on a course of surgery. There were those, too, in other wards, Moffat later explained to Poppy, who did not have flesh wounds but who were troubled with their nerves almost to the point of madness. By the end of the round, Poppy felt that she could have sat down and wept beside each bed at the senselessness of it all.

The group came to what had been the curtained bed and Poppy braced herself once again, but the drape was already half-open and she could see a big, fair, young man with a week's stubble – a trench beard – lying back on the pillows with the covers up around his neck. Poppy, employing the trick that she and Matthews had invented, squinted a little, then slowly brought his face into focus. It appeared to be perfectly regular, thank goodness, with two ears, a normal nose and smiling brown eyes.

'Are you with us this morning, Private Mackay?' Sister asked.

'Aye, I believe I am,' came the reply.

'Private Mackay has lost both arms below the elbow,' Nurse Gallagher said to Poppy. 'He'll have surgery to tidy things up, then he'll probably go to Roehampton to be fitted with new arms.'

'I wondered why he was behind screens,' Poppy said tentatively.

'It was because he only arrived a couple of days back and came in straight from the line. He was utterly exhausted and desperately needed to sleep,' Sister Kay said, overhearing them. She spoke directly to the patient. 'We heard that you got stuck in no-man's-land, Private Mackay.'

'Aye,' said the soldier. Speaking very slowly, he continued, 'I picked up a German grenade and tried to lob it back, but it went off. My pals tried to reach me, but it was awful bad out there.' There was a long pause and then he added, 'I had to lie in the mud and play dead until our stretcher-bearers could come and get me.'

'And now *we've* got you and you're safe,' said Sister Kay.

'Aye, that you have,' he said, giving a sigh. 'When I blacked out, the guns on both sides had been thundering day and night. And when I woke here, between fresh white sheets, with everything so clean and quiet, I thought I must have died and gone to heaven.' He gave an embarrassed laugh. 'Especially since I'm as naked as a newborn.'

Sister nodded. 'You were caked in mud and blood so we had to cut you out of your uniform and wrap you in a blanket.'

'I've not even got my trews!' said the soldier.

Sister smiled and turned to Poppy. 'Pearson, see what you can find in the pyjama box for Private Mackay, will you?'

That night Poppy and Matthews walked down together to catch the bus home.

'I'm fearfully jealous of the amount of hands-on nursing you've done,' Matthews said, after listening to Poppy's tales of the boys of Hut 59. 'I've not been trusted to do so much as take a man's temperature!'

'I'm sure you'll be doing more stuff soon,' Poppy said. She thought of the miles of bloodied bandages that she'd taken on a trolley to the laundry and cringed. 'And when you are doing it, you'll wish you weren't.'

'But mine are all "up" patients. How am I supposed to cultivate a bedside manner when none of them are actually in bed?'

'Your turn will come.'

Matthews looked at Poppy enviously. 'But you've helped those boys. You've done something you can be proud of. All I've done is wash up!'

Back at the hostel, Poppy had a bowl of soup, washed and went to her cubicle. At this time, just before she drifted off to sleep, it was usual for images of Freddie de Vere to flit through her mind. On this occasion, however, the faces of the injured boys of Hut 59 would not be driven out by Freddie de Vere. Round and round they went in her head: snippets of the things they'd said; the singing while their wounds had been dressed; the strangely modulated voice of the band-leader on the gramophone record; the fatigued face of young Thomas; Private Mackay, straight from the front, talking about his trews . . . Vivid slices of her day refused to leave her. It was at once the most shocking, the most dreadful and the most rewarding day of her life.

After lying awake for a couple of hours, she got out her notepad and fountain pen.

6*th* September 1915

Dear Miss Luttrell,

I passed my examinations and I have started working now. I'm sure you've heard of Netley Hut Hospital – it has been set up for war casualties in the fields behind the Royal Victoria. I am working in a hut which is also a ward: a very handsome and well-stocked place with electricity and running water, also a small kitchen, bathroom and store-room. The majority of the food comes over to us from one of the main kitchens and it is usually me who serves it.

I am jolly well exhausted tonight, but I must tell you that I love the work and shall forever be grateful to you for having enough confidence in me to suggest such a thing. To help to save the boys who are saving us is such a privilege; there is so much to do for them and their injuries are mostly very bad.

I hope all is well with you. I think you know that my mother has taken Jane and Mary to live in Wales with my aunt. Aunt Ruby has a small farm with eight horses and six of these have been requisitioned by the military to help transport food and munitions to the front line. Poor Aunt didn't want to part with them, but even horses have to do war work now.

I will now have another try at getting to sleep!
With very best regards and love from

Poppy

Chapter Fourteen

'Do try and keep those Good Eggs at bay a little while longer,' Sister Kay said to Poppy. The two of them glanced outside Hut 59, where two women in sensible coats and old-fashioned felt hats waited patiently for three o'clock and visiting time. 'I see red roses in a basket. And, oh dear, I do believe I can see a pile of religious tracts.'

'But the second woman is carrying a pack of postcards and some pencils,' Poppy said.

'Ah, the boys will like those,' Sister said. '*She* can come in.'

Some weeks had gone by and Poppy was getting to know Sister Kay, who wasn't quite so prickly as she'd thought at first. Or rather, she *was*, but only on behalf of the boys in her ward. She fought to get them extra rations, pleaded for sleeping powders and insisted on having copious amounts of clean linen. Hut 59 had also been one of the first wards in the hospital to get a consignment of blue suits for men who were 'up' patients and who, having had their uniform shot off them on some foreign field, needed something to wear.

'But why do you dislike visitors so much?' Poppy asked her.

'Why? Because they're such time-wasters!' said Sister Kay. 'They disrupt the boys' stability, upset them by saying they can't manage without them and keep asking when they're coming home. They also bring inappropriate presents.'

'That's right!' Moffat said. 'Do you remember the woman who insisted on distributing gloves to every man in the ward, even those without any arms?'

'Quite,' said Sister. 'They put things on the beds – chocolate on my counterpanes! – upset our routines and generally clutter up the place. Haven't you noticed that some of our boys elect to be asleep every afternoon between three and four to try to avoid having to speak to them?'

Poppy nodded that, yes, she had noticed.

'Visitors are very out of place in a hospital,' said Sister Kay. Her eyes scanned the ward, looking for rumpled sheets, pillows not at the peak of puffed-up-ness and untidy locker-tops. 'Pearson, someone's tied a dummy to the end of Thomas's bed. That's going too far. Take it off before visiting time, will you?'

*

By three o'clock there was a queue of these unwanted guests standing at the door. The boys' families came in first, anxiously scanning the ward as they entered to make sure their own particular soldier was still where they'd left him, and then came the Good Eggs. The woman with the basket of red roses insisted on placing a flower and quotation from the Bible on each man's pillow. Poppy, on Sister's instructions, followed behind, collecting up the flowers before they marked the pillowslips, then cutting them shorter and putting them in vases. A man arrived with a pile of that day's newspapers and took one to each bed, but Sister had them quickly moved to the dining table because of the risk of newsprint on the sheets. The boys' favourite of all the visitors was the one who arrived with two crates of locally brewed beer, especially when, following a request from Private Mackay, they were allowed to drink this straight away.

Private Mackay and the other men who were without one or more arms were always looked after first, Poppy had noticed. Usually Smithers or another orderly would appear to give them their breakfasts, or if they were busy else- where, one of the 'up' patients would help out. In return, those with working legs would run an errand for those who weren't so good on their feet, or had no feet at all.

Late that afternoon, Poppy was due to go and cheer on Billy's regiment as they embarked on their journey to France and, with Sister's permission, left Hut 59 at four instead of the usual seven or eight o'clock. She would just have time to go back to the hostel, have a cup of tea and ten minutes' rest with her feet up before going out again.

Wishing the orderly at the YWCA reception desk a good afternoon, she passed through the ground floor and had only reached the stairs when she heard him call that there was a letter for her. Her heart jumped. She'd trained herself not to look in her pigeon-hole because it was just too disappointing when, nine times out of ten, there was nothing there except a note asking her to settle her laundry bill.

She turned, preparing herself for another disappointment, and the orderly handed her the letter. She looked at the writing – it was in a hand she didn't recognise. But there was a regimental crest on the back of the envelope and the letters encircling it said, *Duke of Greystock's Rgt*. Her heart gave an enormous leap. That was *his* unit. The letter was from Freddie.

'There!' said the orderly, seeing her reaction. 'That's put a smile on your face. From your one-and-only, is it?'

Poppy, laughing, said that it might be. With her heart racing she took the letter into the little kitchen upstairs, put it on the shelf and stared at it while she made a pot of tea.

She poured water into the shiny brown teapot, stirred up the leaves and looked at the envelope some more. She mustn't get too excited, she told herself – perhaps he was going to say it wasn't possible for them to meet. Or perhaps he was writing on his mother's instructions in order to sever the ties between them. On the other hand, she thought giddily, perhaps he was going to declare that he loved her and couldn't live without her . . .

But what if her heart got broken right there and then in the YWCA kitchen! Perhaps it was best *not* to open it, to stuff it down the back of a kitchen cabinet and forget all about it. That way she could carry on thinking that he loved her.

Feeling agitated and anxious, she poured the tea and carried cup, saucer and letter back to the cubicle, set the tea on her locker and closed the curtains round the bed in case anyone should arrive back. If it was bad news, she didn't want to have to discuss it. She drank her tea then, half-scared and half-hopeful, snatched up the envelope and opened it quickly, before she could change her mind.

Duke of Greystock's Regiment

8ᵗʰ September 1915

Dear Poppy,
I have been thinking of you – don't dream that I haven't been. I have also been learning how to be a soldier, though, and my superiors have seen that this has taken precedence over everything else. When we get back to our quarters at night, I think about writing to you, but fall asleep within moments, before I can even lift a pen.

As we all anticipated, the regiment is being posted overseas. There was a rumour that we were going to Gallipoli, and this would not have been good as I speak no Turkish, but it turns out that we are going where we are most needed: northern France. As I speak a little French – enough, perhaps, to get me out of trouble – this is what I had hoped for.

Dear little Poppy, I have often thought of our last meeting and how happy I was to find that your feelings seemed to reflect my own. I think we have much to talk about . . . I don't want to be alarmist, but in these days of uncertainty, when goodbye might mean forever, there are things I would like to speak of before I go to fight. The death of my brother alerted me to such niceties; if I'd known that I was never going to see him again there was so much I would have said to him.

We have been granted several days' home leave and then we go from England, via Southampton, on 28th October. If you would still like to meet up, perhaps you could get an afternoon's leave on the 27th and we can go for tea at the Criterion? I had hoped that we could go dancing or do something gay, but – forgive me – I have a regimental dinner to attend that night.

Can we meet at the Criterion at three o'clock? Will you let me know? I will wait impatiently to hear.
With my love,

Freddie

Poppy read the letter five more times and then left the hostel with it in her pocket. He'd written to her – he'd actually written! He wanted to meet her. He was going to take her to tea. He wanted to speak to her seriously . . .

As usual, a fair amount of people had gathered between the station and the docks in order to wave off another regiment of young men going to war. Some were local residents who regarded turning out to cheer as part of their war work. Others had come from a distance to say goodbye to a member of their family. Some were good-time girls who wanted not only to give a handsome soldier-boy a smacking kiss, but also to get his address and send him a few saucy pin-up photographs.

Poppy heard someone saying that Billy's regiment was forming-up by the station, so positioned herself on a street corner in order to get the best views. If she hadn't been in uniform, she thought, she would have climbed on to a garden wall in order to see better, but the thought of Sister Kay discovering that one of her VADs had behaved in such an unseemly manner stopped her.

Joining the people milling about waving flags, Poppy realised that she ought to have bought something to give to Billy, but, hurrying into a corner shop, found that everyone had had the same idea and they had completely sold out of cigarettes and chocolate bars. Going back to her place on the corner, she heard, in the distance, the sounds of a regimental band playing a marching tune, men's voices singing, and the *stamp-stamp-stamp* of heavily booted feet. When a wave of khaki appeared around the corner, her heart swelled with pride. Our Billy, marching off to glory!

The regiment marched on and suddenly she wasn't thinking about glory, but of her own wounded men in Hut 59, and of the limbs lost, bodies mangled, blood spilled and lives changed forever. The shattered men in the hospital, though, were the fortunate ones, the ones who'd come back. Thinking of Billy in relation to the boys she nursed made her eyes fill with stinging tears. Her brother – her own brother – was marching away! What if he returned without limbs, as some of her boys had done? What if he didn't return at all?

The men, marching six abreast behind the band and singing, whistling or just smiling broadly at the reception they were getting from the crowd, reached where Poppy was standing. As they went by, girls waved and cheered, threw flowers or pressed rouged lips to a manly cheek. Some gave them little gifts, such as woolly mufflers or thick socks, for the coming winter was predicted to be bitter.

At last, when two thirds of the column had gone by, she saw Billy on the outside of his six, marching towards her. He had a carnation sticking out of the barrel of his rifle, three notes pinned to his shoulder epaulettes and his pockets were bulging with things he'd been given. Poppy, waiting for him to reach where she was standing, didn't think she'd ever seen him so broad of shoulder, walking so tall, looking quite so pleased with himself.

She stepped off the kerb and waved, then called his name.

He turned, his smile growing even wider. 'Hiya, sis!'

She ran along beside him as much as the crowd would allow her to do. 'Isn't this *grand*!' she said. 'And I'm sorry I didn't buy you anything, but when you get to France, you can write and let me know what you're short of.'

'Will do!' Billy said. 'What a turnout, eh? It's been like this all the way from London – people waving and cheering as the train went through stations. Whenever it stopped, girls got on and gave us cocoa or buns, or newspapers and ciggies.'

Poppy laughed – he looked so happy with everything.

'Tell Ma you've seen me, eh?' Billy said as the band began playing *Tipperary* and the men increased pace a little. 'Tell her that I looked the part, won't you?'

'I will,' Poppy promised. 'She'll be right proud of you. And I'm proud too, Billy!'

But he was gone, swallowed up by the lines of men.

Poppy waited until the whole regiment had gone past, the front of their line had reached the gates of the Docks, and the well-wishers who'd gathered to cheer the men on were dispersing. It was odd, she thought, that when the soldiers disappeared, the cheering and flag waving stopped too, and those left in the street just melted away. It was like the end of a show; the performance was over . . .

YWCA Hostel,
Southampton

12th September 1915

Dearest Ma,

I have just seen our Billy! He marched right past me, enormously pleased with himself, covered all over with love tokens from girls. He said I must be sure to let you know I'd seen him. I don't know the name of the ship he's on or the port they are heading for, but it's only an overnight journey and – let's pray they are speaking the truth – they say our shipping lanes are well protected by the Navy.

How are you, Ma, and the girls? I'm glad you have all settled in with Aunt Ruby. I think that is by far the safest place for you. Yes, do consider staying down there for the duration of the war.

I am sorry I haven't written more, but it is such awfully hard work being a VAD and when I'm not working I'm asleep. I do love my work at Netley, though. Sister is strict, but adores the men and gives them such tender care we cannot help but emulate her. Some of our boys have no arms and I have had to learn how to shave them. There is a gigantic Scot, Private Mackay, whose arms were blown off by a bomb, and I was terrified shaving him in case I cut him, but he was so good and quiet when I was doing it and afterwards thanked me in such a heartfelt way that I had to go outside and weep. The boys – that is, the regular Tommies (the officers are always 'the men') –

rarely complain. The standard reply when asked how they are is 'not too bad' or 'in the pink'. They are just pleased to be home – and be alive.

Ma, I can't resist telling you this, but don't breathe a word to anyone. You remember the younger de Vere boy, Freddie? We have become quite close and he has written to me to ask me to meet him for afternoon tea at the Criterion when he comes through Southampton. I like him very much so I am fearfully excited about this!

I have an early start in the morning so will close now, with lots of love to you, Aunt Ruby, Jane and Mary, from your daughter.

Poppy

She finished the letter, put it in an envelope, thought about things, then opened the letter and took out the second page containing the piece about Freddie de Vere. Her mother would not understand, she decided. She wouldn't think it was right. She probably hadn't heard how society was changing. She took a fresh piece of paper and rewrote the second page without mentioning him.

Finally, after getting ready for bed, she put Freddie's letter under her pillow, hoping to drift off to sleep and dream of him. When she closed her eyes, the figure who came unwanted into her head was the elegant one of Miss Cardew. Where did she figure in their relationship?

Chapter Fifteen

'I say, girls, listen to this from the personal column,' said Jameson. She read out from the newspaper she was holding: *'A young lady, who was engaged to be married to an officer killed at Ypres, is willing to dedicate her life to any soldier blinded or severely incapacitated as a result of the war.'*

Poppy and Matthews were silent for a moment. It was seven in the morning and they were sitting together in the hostel canteen having breakfast.

'Gosh,' Poppy said then. 'She's taking a risk. She could end up with *anyone.*'

'Of course she could,' Jameson said. 'And that's just it. She's admitting that because the man she loves is dead, she doesn't care what happens to her. How *terrible.*'

'But don't you think the new chap will mind being second best?' Matthews asked. 'She's obviously still in love with the one who died.'

The other two shook their heads wonderingly.

'And it would be difficult if the one who died was a colonel or something and the new one was a private,' Jameson said. 'He'd never feel quite up to scratch, poor lamb.' She took a spoonful of porridge, turned the page and began studying the *Died in Action* lists.

'Anyway, Jameson, how are your Hun?' Matthews suddenly asked.

Jameson frowned. 'Don't call them that.'

'Your Germans, then.'

'*You* were calling them Hun before you started nursing them,' Poppy pointed out.

Jameson began to protest, but on both girls insisting that indeed she had, she said *that* was before she knew what they were like.

'And what *are* they like?' Matthews enquired.

'Just like us. They really *are*, though,' she added after a moment. 'They simply speak another language.'

'But aren't they terribly fierce and violent?' Poppy asked. 'That's what the newspapers are always saying.'

Jameson shook her head. 'They have to say that so that people want to go out and shoot them. Actually, the ones at the hospital are very polite and extremely grateful for everything we do for them.' Looking at her two friends rather sheepishly, she added, 'They're far from home, they miss their families and they're scared to death about what might happen to them if their country is defeated. They're just like us!'

'Maybe,' Poppy said with doubt in her voice.

'The ward is guarded day and night,' Jameson went on, 'and they're not allowed as much as a sniff of fresh air. When they're well enough to leave hospital they'll go straight to a prison camp. They may never see their families again.'

'Well,' Matthews said, 'that's their fault.'

'Their fault for being German?' responded Jameson.

Matthews shrugged. 'Yes, I suppose that's what I mean.'

'It's what happens in a war,' Poppy said. 'There are always different sides. There's you and there's them, and someone's got to win.'

'But they're just really nice men,' Jameson went on. 'They're all officers – *honourable* prisoners of war. They kiss my hand when I go off duty; they're interested in my family and what I do in my spare time. One of them even gave me a box of German chocolates.'

Noticing the look in her eye and the tone of her voice, Poppy nudged Matthews. 'What's he look like – the one who gave you chocolates?' she asked Jameson.

'Oh, he's very good-looking,' Jameson said immediately. 'Thick fair hair and a strong jawline, quite tanned. He hasn't got blue eyes, though – they're a greeny-hazel.' She suddenly noticed that both girls were looking at her with raised eyebrows. '*What?*'

Poppy and Matthews just smiled.

'It's not like that – not like that at all!'

'I should think not,' said Matthews.

*

That morning, Poppy made up her mind to ask Sister Kay if she could have the afternoon of the twenty-seventh off. She hadn't asked before because she couldn't decide if she should tell Sister the truth – that she was going out with a man – and risk being forbidden to go. The other thing was, once she had permission then she'd have to write to Freddie, and she hadn't been able to decide what sort of a letter this should be. How much should she say about her feelings? Should she ask about Miss Cardew?

Going into Hut 59 that morning, Poppy found it quieter than usual. This was normally a sign that there had been a death or some sort of emergency on the ward, and she looked around anxiously to make sure her favourites were still there. She cared deeply about all the boys, of course, but certain of them had touched her heart. Young Thomas, especially . . . She looked towards his bed, but he was still in it, the small brown bear hanging from the end bar. Private Mackay was in place, too, and Private Franklin and one or two others she took a special interest in.

'Why is everyone so hushed?' she asked Moffat when she stopped for a breather in between delivering the breakfast trays.

Moffat looked rueful. 'It's so sad. Private Taylor has heard that his twin brother has been killed in Flanders. He was gassed and then shot.'

Poppy gave a gasp of horror.

Moffat nodded. 'Both sides are using poisonous gas now. The Allies released the gas, but the wind was blowing the wrong way and it drifted back on to them.'

'What about their gas masks?'

'They say they're no good – they fog up and you can't breathe properly in them. Taylor's brother became blinded by gas, stumbled on to barbed wire and got tangled up. There he was for Fritz, a sitting target.'

Moffat moved off to start changing beds and left on her own in the kitchen waiting for the porridge to arrive, Poppy sipped water until the lump in her throat had gone. Imagine losing a brother; imagine losing your *twin*.

After breakfast she asked about having the afternoon off and Sister Kay, distracted by the imminent arrival of Private Taylor's family, agreed without questioning her about what she was going to do.

Moffat, who'd overheard, later said, 'If you're meeting a man – fine, go ahead. Just don't let anyone from the hospital see you.'

'I *am* meeting a man,' said Poppy, unable to resist the joy of telling someone else.

'A Tommy?'

'No,' Poppy said, trying not to sound too proud. 'An officer. Duke of Greystock's Regiment.'

'Oh dear,' Moffat said.

'Why "oh dear"? Do you know something about that regiment?'

'No, it's just that you sound as if you might be a bit soppy about him.' She raised her eyebrows. 'Take a tip from me, old girl: don't fall for any nonsense he might give you about needing to seize the moment in case "something happens" and you never see each other again.'

Poppy thought back to Freddie's letter, which she knew by heart. Could it be that his intentions weren't honourable? She felt rather thrillingly alarmed, then realised that he'd have very little opportunity to behave immorally during afternoon tea at the Criterion.

'I don't mean to play the maiden aunt,' Moffat went on, 'but I just want to warn you to be careful. Some men will play on a girl's emotions to get her between the sheets. Other men might be perfectly sincere but might go off to war and never return. Either way you stand a good chance of getting your heart broken.'

'Have you had . . . ?'

Moffat nodded, pressed her lips together and said no more.

There was precious little space to get away from everyone in Hut 59, but Sister had Private Taylor moved to a reclining chair near the nursing station at the top of the ward and had screens put around it. When his mother and father arrived, pale and worn-looking, he broke down completely and Sister asked Moffat and Poppy to go to the opposite end of the ward and get as many of the boys as possible involved in piecing together one of the huge jigsaws that had been donated.

Visiting time came and went, but Private Taylor's family stayed on, and only left when it was time to catch their train back to Leicester.

Before Poppy left that day, the 'Thames by Tower Bridge' jigsaw not yet completed, Sister Kay beckoned her over.

'I'm slightly worried about our Thomas,' she said. 'He's been so upset by Private Taylor's loss.'

Poppy nodded. Thomas's bed was next to that of Private Taylor, who'd been acting as a kind of temporary uncle to the boy. Since he'd heard the news of his twin, however, Taylor had hardly spoken to anyone.

'Thomas goes for surgery next week and, well, he's a sad little chap. It would make all the difference if his mother could come in and see him.'

'She's in Newcastle, isn't she?'

Sister nodded. 'I've written to her, but she's not replied. I've managed to get her a free travel pass now, though. I thought Thomas could write asking her to visit and send the pass at the same time.'

'Do you want me to help him write it?'

'I want you to write it for him,' Sister said drily. 'The lad can't pen much more than his name – and he's nowhere near recruitment age, either. God alone knows what he's doing in the army.'

When Poppy went over to Thomas with a pad and pencil, he was half-hidden under a pile of blankets. She tidied his bed and changed his pillowslip, then told him she had a travel warrant ready to send to his mother. 'So,

Sister wants us to write her a nice letter to go with it, Thomas. What shall we say?'

The boy looked at her with dull eyes. 'She won't come. She's got three babbies at home.'

'Your little brothers and sister?' Poppy asked. 'How old are they?'

'The babby is six months, Georgie is two and Flora is five.'

'Perhaps your da can look after them for a day?'

'My own da is dead,' said Thomas. 'The three bairns are from her new man an' he's in the factory working nights.' His eyes filled with sudden tears and he turned his head so that Poppy wouldn't see them. 'He wouldna let her come and see me anyhow. He doesna like me.'

Poppy took his hand and squeezed it. 'I'm sure he does! He's probably just a very busy man, earning money to feed all those babbies.' She brandished the notebook. 'Now, what do you want to say to her?'

Thomas pushed his face into the pillow. 'Nothin'. She won't come.'

'Thomas . . .' Poppy said wheedlingly. *Dear Ma*, she wrote, and waited. 'Come on, Thomas, I've got to say something.'

Thomas gave a great sigh. 'Dear Ma, I hope this finds you as well as it leaves me,' he said in a monotone. 'I am in hospital at the moment, but will soon be back fighting for our country. Goodbye. From your son, Thomas.'

'But that's not true, is it?' Poppy said. 'You know you won't be sent back to France, not with one leg. Does she know about your leg, Thomas?'

The boy gave a nod. 'Doesn't matter – she won't come,' he said. 'Put what I said.'

Poppy, beginning to write, said aloud, 'Dear Ma, I hope this finds you as well as it leaves me. I am in hospital at the moment, but will soon be back fighting for our country.'

What she actually wrote, however, her pen scudding along the lined pad, was:

Dear Mrs Stilgoe,
Please forgive my writing to you, but I am a VAD at Netley Hut Hospital, where Thomas is an especial favourite amongst both the nurses and the other boys in Hut 59. He is rather low at the moment and as he has a surgical procedure to face soon, we believe he would dearly love to see you. We are sending a travel warrant in the hope that you will be able to use it.
Kind regards,

Poppy Pearson, VAD,
On behalf of Sister Kay, Hut 59

Chapter Sixteen

YWCA Hostel,
Southampton

10th October 1915

Dear Freddie,
Thank you for your letter. I do hope you and your family are well and perhaps slowly coming to terms with the terrible loss of your brother.

I am so sorry I didn't reply immediately to your invitation. I wasn't sure what the hospital rules were about going out with the opposite sex (we are highly protected hothouse flowers here!), but in the end Sister gave me the afternoon off and didn't enquire what I was doing, which saved me having to tell her a fib. I'd love to meet you for afternoon tea.

Freddie, can I be really bold? I think about you a great deal and, since you kissed me outside the church, feel that *our relationship is more than just a friendship. If this is so, then there is something I dearly want to speak to you about when we meet. It concerns Miss Cardew. There! I have been very bold and will leave you to guess exactly what my question is.*

I am very excited about seeing you and will meet you at the Criterion on the 27th at three o'clock. In the meantime, I think about you every day and hope with all my heart that you come through the war unscathed.
With love,

Poppy

'Do you think *"with love"* is the right sign-off for a letter to Freddie?' Poppy asked Matthews over breakfast.

Matthews nodded. '*"With love"* is fine. *"All my love"* would be too much and *"Yours sincerely"* not enough.'

'Oh good,' Poppy said. 'That was about my tenth try. I was sitting up for hours trying to work out what I wanted to say.' She sealed down the envelope. 'There – I can't change it now, and anyway, I've run out of notepaper.'

'The Criterion it is, then,' Matthews said. 'How terribly posh! What are you going to wear?'

Going into the ward that morning, Poppy saw immediately that changes had been made by the night staff. A dining table had been removed and four more injured men had been admitted overnight, so four more beds and lockers had been squeezed into what was already a crowded ward.

'It'll be bed rest for our new chaps,' Nurse Gallagher said, sliding screens around where they lay. 'We'll monitor them and change their bandages if we have to, but let them sleep for as long as they like.'

'Is this the most patients you've ever had in here?' Poppy asked.

Nurse Gallagher shook her head. 'Oh no,' she said. 'After Ypres last October we had so many men coming in they had to lie on mattresses between the beds. We even had some patients balanced on stretchers along the dining table. Sixty-eight men, at one count.'

'Never!'

'All the surgical wards were the same.'

Poppy, trying to imagine how she'd ever get the trays out if she had sixty-eight men to look after, was about to go into the kitchen to begin breakfast duties, when a young man in a white coat came into the ward with some paperwork in his hand. Recognising him as the doctor she'd met on her second day, Poppy felt her cheeks turning pink.

'I believe you have four new chaps here,' he said, then looked at Poppy more closely and smiled. 'It's Pearson, isn't it?'

Poppy drew herself to attention, as VADs were meant to do when greeted by an officer of a higher rank. 'Yes, sir. VAD Pearson.'

'Well, Pearson, I believe you have four new casualties here under Doctor Armstrong's care?' On Poppy confirming this, he added, 'Or perhaps you've found an orderly who could operate on them?'

Poppy hid a smile. How beastly of him to make reference to her blunder! But he was smiling, too, so how could she take offence?

'Sorry, that was rather tactless,' he said. 'Let's start again. There are four new patients here under Doctor Armstrong's care. Have they had their initial assessment yet?'

Poppy shook her head. 'No. They're being monitored, but Sister Kay wants them to sleep as long as they like before they get messed about with.'

'"*Messed about with*?"' he repeated, raising his eyebrows. 'That's what you think of our leading war injury consultant's care, is it?'

'Sorry, I didn't mean . . .' But she saw that he was joking.

He looked over at the boys in the nearby beds who were watching the two of them with considerable interest. 'I believe your patients are trying to overhear our conversation, Pearson.'

'Yes, sir,' Poppy replied. 'The morning newspapers aren't in yet – they're looking for some diversion.'

'I get the feeling that they're taking notes.'

'Sorry,' Poppy said. 'They do all love a bit of gossip. They're always wanting to hear if someone's got an assignation, if there's been a tiff between two orderlies or if Sister Kay has fallen out with one of the Good Eggs – the visitors, I mean,' she amended quickly.

'Well, I feel rather sorry we can't give them anything more interesting to watch,' he said.

Poppy, uncertain of his meaning, didn't reply.

'Well,' he continued after a moment, looking down at his top sheet and making a series of ticks, 'will you please tell Sister Kay that Doctor Armstrong's team will visit at two o'clock this afternoon?'

'Certainly, sir,' Poppy said.

'And my name's Michael. Michael Archer,' he said. Slightly shocked (imagine what Sister would say if she called a doctor by his first name!), Poppy didn't say anything further, but was unable to prevent herself smiling. He grinned back at her and went out.

The moment the swing door shut behind him there was a chorus of wolf whistles from the boys in the beds and a hail of questions.

'Is he your new sweetheart, Nurse?'

'Kept him quiet, didn't you?'

'Does your mother know you're out?'

'For goodness sake!' Poppy said. 'You're all being *very* silly. I've only ever seen him once before in my life!'

'Once in your life, but always in your dreams!' someone called, and there were hoots of laughter.

'Look, will you please stop . . . I hardly know his name!' Poppy protested.

'I expect you just call him *"darling"*!' shouted Private Mackay, and the gale of guffaws which accompanied this made Nurse Gallagher stop her round and come to see what was going on.

'Sorry,' Poppy murmured. 'They all seem to be in very high spirits today.'

174

'Really, Pearson?' Nurse Gallagher looked at her with raised eyebrows. 'And it's nothing to do with you, I suppose?'

Just before dinner time, one hundred pairs of red-striped pyjamas arrived as a gift from a factory in Winchester that Sister Kay had been corresponding with. She wanted the boys to put them on straight away and be smart for visiting time, so a pair was allotted to each injured soldier. The old, over-washed and ill-matched pyjamas were then parcelled up ready to be sent to one of the new private convalescent hospitals which were springing up all over the place.

When Doctor Armstrong and his team came in briefly at two o'clock, all the men were looking smart in the new pyjamas, but Poppy was in the kitchen doing the wash-ing-up and therefore missed seeing her new friend again.

Going back to the hostel that night, she found a letter in her pigeon-hole.

hole in back of beyond.

Dear Sis,
This is a shit hole you will have to excuse the expression but that is the only way i can discribe it. I never new it would be like this or i wouldn't of come. I cant tell you were we are they dont tell us nothing, all I can tell you is we got on the ship and i was as sick as a pig all the way

across to france. From the port we were herded in cattle trucks all day and night to somewhere they havent told us the name of.

It has rained ever since we got here and I have not changed my clothes or slept for five nights because of the guns going off everywhere enough to drive a chap mad. Yesterday we were moved nearer to the fighting and they say that tomorrow it will be our turn to support the front line and we will be climbing out of the trenches and running towards the jerries and trying to bayonet anyone we meet. They tell you to run and thats it, you have to do it or they shoot you. Of the men who went yesterday half of the troop were shot down by jerries straight away and those who did get further were torn to bits by the barbed wire (what they were told would be already cut for them), or had their arms and legs shot off. The boys say that there is a surgery back behind the Line where they cut your mangled limbs off you and they have to work so quickly theres no time to dispose of them and they are just left in piles in the corridor. I probly shouldnt be writing this but i dont care if the censer catches me, they might lock me up and i will be out of it.

I tell you, this place is worse than hell. Sometimes if you die out there in the mud they cant get you back. Anyway its not worth getting you back because your in so many parts. They put a cross up for you it says RIP which the boys say means Ripped In Pieces.

There are officers looking at you all the time to make sure you fight. If you fall over into the mud and lay there pretending your injured they no and you get shot by firing squad the next day.

Why is it everyone says they want to come here and fight? I have to get out of it or i will go mad. I do not think i will see the month out. i am thinking of running off it is all to much for anyone to take.

Billy

Chapter Seventeen

'Now, have you decided what you're going to wear to meet this officer of yours?' Matthews asked.

She, Poppy and Jameson – all starving after a full day on the wards – were in the YWCA canteen having a cup of soup and a sandwich. The sandwich was a cheese one, though it contained such a small amount of cheese that it was barely worthy of its name, for they were cutting back on food almost everywhere.

'What to wear? Not yet,' Poppy said.

Since she'd had the letter from Billy she hadn't thought of anything much except her brother and what would become of him. She'd told Matthews a little about the contents of his letter, but was too bitterly ashamed to tell anyone else. Imagine if any of the boys of Hut 59, with all their bravely borne war wounds, discovered that their VAD's brother was about to abandon his pals and run off in the middle of battle! It was lucky

178

indeed that the censor hadn't read the letter or Billy would surely be under arrest already.

She should have known that something like this would happen, she thought – that the brave, strutting Billy she'd seen marching off to engage with the enemy wasn't the real Billy, but a sham got up to charm the girls. She pictured him as she'd last seen him, swaggering down the high street, tossing his head this way and that and winking at anyone who took his fancy. How quickly things had changed.

'I think that a quite formal day dress would be appropriate for afternoon tea at the Criterion,' Jameson said. 'Maybe a small, close-fitting hat . . .'

'I thought I'd just wear my uniform.'

Two cries of protest rang out.

'For a start,' Jameson said, 'you don't want to be seen as a VAD by anyone else there. Remember, that we aren't supposed to *date*, as the Americans put it.'

'And you should look delightfully feminine and desirable,' said Matthews. 'Your uniform suits you, but up till now Freddie has always seen you looking quite regular and ordinary, first as a servant and then as a nurse.'

'Gosh, I almost forgot. You were the de Veres' *maid*, weren't you?' said Jameson in a tone of amused horror, and got kicked under the table by Matthews. 'Well, anything you want to borrow of mine, you can,' she added swiftly.

Poppy sighed. It all took such a lot of thinking about. Everyone loved a VAD, of course, so she'd presumed she'd just go in her uniform, but now she realised that that wouldn't be quite right. She didn't want to be a perfect angel of a nurse – she wanted Freddie to long for her as she longed for him. She wanted to look at least as desirable as Miss Cardew.

'You should wear your hair down,' Jameson advised. 'Men like long hair.'

'That's true,' said Matthews. She and Poppy exchanged meaningful glances. 'Jameson, you've been wearing your hair down rather a lot lately, haven't you?'

Jameson said nothing, but her cheeks went pink.

'I've got some rouge and some lip balm,' Matthews said to Poppy. 'Put a spot of colour on your cheeks first, and then mix a little of the rouge with the balm – it will make your lips a lovely shade of pink.'

Poppy said, 'Sister Malcolm told us that lipstick is . . .'

'The devil's work!' Matthews finished. 'Never mind – you're not going out with her.'

Jameson said she didn't have many clothes with her, but she certainly had a more extensive wardrobe than the other two girls. When they went upstairs, Poppy tried on first an evening dress in silver ('Just too much!' Matthews declared), then two rather flouncy afternoon dresses and a stylish two-piece fitted costume in a dark purple.

'It's exactly right on you!' Jameson declared of the latter.

'And very à la mode with the shorter skirt,' Matthews said, for it was, rather daringly, of mid-calf length.

'Freddie de Vere won't be able to resist falling in love with you.'

'Here are some kid-leather gloves,' said Jameson, putting them on the bed. 'And what about this?' She brought out a cream pill-box hat with a little spotted veil and settled it on Poppy's head.

'Lovely!' both the girls agreed.

Poppy, thanking them both, made a vow to concentrate on the coming excitement and try to forget about Billy for a couple of days. She wasn't out there with him and she couldn't play the big sister now. She just had to hope that he would come to his senses, do the decent thing and fight like everyone else.

'This will be Private James's tenth operation,' Moffat said as, the next day, she and Poppy blanket-bathed the young soldier ready for his visit to the operating theatre. This was a job which was mostly carried out by male orderlies, but that morning Smithers had joined a group who'd gone to the docks to collect injured soldiers from a troopship.

'His tenth?' Poppy said, wincing a little on his behalf.

'They've been trying to tidy up his remaining leg. That's right, isn't it, Private James?'

'That's what they *say* they're doing,' Private James said dolefully, 'but I reckon they're slicing me up and selling me down the butcher's as rump steak.'

Moffat, deftly moving towels around in order to preserve Private James's modesty, smiled sympathetically.

Poppy tried to smile too, but the mashed-up leg before her was so revolting that she found this almost impossible. It was not merely the sight of the leg, but the smell that came from it, for gangrene had set in during the time it had taken to get him to safety, and the awful stink of rotting flesh made her feel nauseous. His other leg had gone completely, right up to the thigh bone, so the surgeons were doing what they could to save the remainder of this one.

Once Private James's battered leg had been cleaned up and made ready for the surgeons, there were three other patients to bathe and prepare for surgery that day. One of these was Thomas, who was having an operation on what was left of his leg.

'He's lucky he didn't get gangrene, too,' Moffat said. 'And at least he's got one good leg, whatever happens to this one. Not like poor Private James.'

'There's been no word from Thomas's mother yet?' Poppy asked in a low voice.

Moffat shook her head. 'Nothing. Maybe she just can't cope with seeing him so badly injured. Some of them can't, you know.'

'But he's only a kid. He *needs* her.'

'I know. It's so sad . . .'

They reached Thomas's bed and, though they both greeted him cheerily, received no reply.

'How are you feeling, Thomas?' Moffat asked.

By way of an answer, Thomas just turned awkwardly in the bed and hunched himself away from them.

'Pearson and I are here to get you ready for the surgeon,' Moffat said.

Silence.

'Aren't you speaking to us, Thomas?'

There was a long moment, then he said gruffly, 'No point. I've seen the grey lady and I won't be here much longer.'

Moffat sighed. 'Really, Thomas, who's been telling you such silly nonsense?'

'Who's he talking about?' Poppy asked.

Moffat tutted. 'The grey lady is supposed to be the ghost of a nurse.' She put her arms out, ghost-like, and affected a blank face. 'Lots of hospitals are supposed to have them – lady ghosts who walk the corridors at night. It's quite ridiculous, of course.' She sniffed. 'I wouldn't mind if they came in and did something useful – rolled bandages or washed out the bedpans – but just to walk up and down corridors . . .'

'They're omens of death,' Thomas said in a hoarse voice. 'The sergeant who died told me about her – he saw the grey lady and that was the end of him. Private Taylor's seen her and now he knows *he's* going to die and join his twin. He says he's looking forward to it.'

Poppy gave Moffat an enquiring look. 'Is Private Taylor speaking now?'

'Only about dying,' Moffat said under her breath.

'The grey lady came here last night,' Thomas said. 'She walked down the centre of the ward – well, she drifted, more like, all grey and misty. An' when she got to the end of my bed she stopped an' just looked at me. If she comes for me tonight I'm going to go with her.'

'Thomas, your operation isn't life-threatening,' Moffat said. 'That's why you're going down to the theatre last. The surgeons are just going to make a tidy job of your leg and clean up any remaining shrapnel wounds.'

'Maybe I'll just drift off and die while I'm under the anaesthetic an' she'll come and get me.'

'You didn't see a grey lady – you had a nightmare,' Moffat said soothingly. 'It was just a bad dream.'

'What did you have for supper that might have brought it on?' Poppy asked, trying to think back. 'Was it cheese?'

'It *wasn't* a dream,' Thomas said. 'I tell you, it was the grey lady. An' if she comes tonight I'm gonna go with her.'

'Well, I shall fetch you back!' Poppy said.

When they'd finished getting Thomas ready, Moffat told Sister what he'd said and Poppy was asked if she wouldn't mind sitting with him for a couple of hours when he came back to the ward after his operation.

'He won't be awake for a while,' Sister said, 'so if you could just stay on until he comes round properly it would be a real help. We don't want him going after any grey ladies and falling out of bed.'

'I'd be happy to stay,' Poppy said.

'Good lass. Thank you,' Sister said warmly. 'I'm sure the night staff would look after him, but . . .'

'I know,' Poppy nodded, basking in the light of Sister Kay's praise. 'But they don't know him like we do.'

The other men who'd been down for operations had woken up at various points, been given painkillers and gone off to sleep again before Thomas came back from the theatre. When the night staff came on, Poppy put a wooden stool in the space next to Thomas's bed and sat there sewing buttons on shirts.

By nine o'clock, most of the ward was asleep and the place was almost silent. Thomas had not come round from the anaesthetic yet, although he was breathing steadily and his colour was better than it had been earlier. Poppy, looking at him closely, began to wonder how long it would be before he woke and, thinking longingly of her bed, wondered if she might get a lift home with one of the orderlies.

The two night VADs at the nursing station – girls who worked elsewhere during the day but did voluntary work at night – were bent over the desk, doing paperwork. The lamps in the ward had been turned down. Outside the hut, their footsteps muffled by the grass, people went by the windows with torches or lanterns, their shadows briefly flickering across the walls. The patients in their beds breathed evenly, snored gently, and the ward grew more still. It had, Poppy thought, something of the hushed solemnity and gravity of a church about it – and thinking that, she suddenly felt overwhelmed with pity for the young men within their care, these boys whose lives would be changed irrevocably by the wounds they bore.

She was aware of wisps of fog seeping in through the windows. When someone opened the door at the far end of the ward, a cloud of mist came in too, for the river wasn't far away and the huts had been built on meadowland.

Poppy heard footsteps trip-trapping down the wooden floor and looked up from her needlework. As she did so, a figure stopped at the end of Thomas's bed and the light from an outside lamp illuminated the lady in grey standing there.

Startled, Poppy gave a little cry and dropped a shirt on the floor.

'Sorry!' said the grey one in a whisper. 'I didn't mean to alarm you. I was just passing through on my way to see the night staff and saw you sitting there.'

'I'm waiting for a patient to come round from surgery.'

The other girl smiled and nodded. 'Well, goodnight to you.'

'Wait!' Poppy whispered back. 'Do you come along here often?'

The girl nodded. 'Every night. I'm from the surgeons' office. I log the number of men operated on each day.'

'And you're a St John nurse?' Poppy asked, knowing that although the Red Cross VADs wore blue dresses, the St John nurses always wore grey.

'That's right.'

'Ah! Thomas here thought you were the grey lady come to get him.'

'Well, I'm not dead yet!' the girl said, smiling as she went on her way.

Poppy checked on Thomas's breathing and felt his pulse. Why wasn't he awake yet? She couldn't stay by his side all night! She had to work the following morning *and* look her best to meet Freddie in the afternoon.

She picked up the shirt from the floor and, as she did so, thought she saw a flicker of movement from Thomas's eye, as if he'd taken the opportunity to peep at her.

'Thomas!' she whispered. 'Are you awake?'

No reply came.

'I'm just going to talk to the night staff about you.' Leaving the shirts on the bed, Poppy went to the nursing station, not sure whether Thomas was asleep or just pretending to be.

'What do you think?' she asked the VADs, and went on to explain about Thomas and how he'd said he might not return to consciousness after the operation, but drift away with the grey lady. 'I don't know if he's come round properly. Shall I go and find a doctor?'

'Begging your pardon.' There was a voice behind Poppy, and she turned to see that a plump, no-nonsense sort of a woman had appeared while she'd been speaking. 'I think you're talking about my lad.'

'Thomas?' Poppy asked in surprise. 'Thomas Stilgoe? Are you Mrs Stilgoe?'

The woman nodded and put down the suitcase she'd been carrying. 'Well, I was till I married Mr Lambert.'

'I wrote to you . . . My name's Pearson.'

'I got your letter, pet, and thank you for it,' said the visitor. 'I would've got here sooner but had a deal to do to farm out the brood at home, and the babby wasn't well, either. I started off early this morning but the train was diverted and I thought I'd never get here.' She paused for breath. 'But what's wrong with my bonny lad?'

'Nothing at all. Well, his leg, of course, which you know about. He had an operation on it this afternoon and we've been waiting for him to come round.'

'What was that about a grey lady?'

'Oh, he had some idea in his head that there was a grey lady coming for him – a ghost! And he said he was going to go with her.'

'Stuff and nonsense!' said Thomas's mother stoutly.

Poppy pointed out his bed and Mrs Lambert went over. 'Thomas! Whatever are you playing at?' she asked in a loud whisper. 'Wake up, pet!'

There was a squeal of surprise from the bed. 'Ma?' Thomas said. 'Ma! Is it *you*?'

'Well, it's not some grey lady ghost! Now wake up and let these nice nurses see that you're all right.'

'But . . . how did you get here?'

'Steam trains and Shanks's pony. How d'you think?'

Thomas struggled to sit up, but continued to regard his mother doubtfully.

'I'm surprised at you, Thomas, I really am – leading these lasses such a song and dance!'

Poppy came along with an enamel bowl in case Thomas was sick. 'Will you be staying here tonight, Mrs Lambert?' she asked.

'Aye, that I will, pet,' said the lady. 'They're putting me up in a nice little visitors' room. And tomorrow, with your say-so, we'll both say thank you kindly and goodbye.'

'Well, I don't know if you can go just like that,' Poppy began, taken aback. 'I think you have to get discharge papers.'

'Oh, I'll sort that right enough, pet,' said Mrs Lambert. 'My Thomas is only fifteen, see. He should never have been allowed to join the army in the first place. I went and told the recruiting officer but he wouldn't take any notice, so I've come to take him home meself!'

Chapter Eighteen

Looking up at the Criterion Hotel as she approached it, Poppy felt quite overawed, despite knowing that Jameson's suit was most becoming, her fingernails were buffed until they shone and she was, daringly, wearing a little of Matthews's pink rouge on her lips.

The hotel was built in the classical style with marble columns and niches containing statues, and there was a grand circle of steps leading up to its entrance. A row of bay trees, trailing patriotic red, white and blue ribbons, stood along the front of the building, and a man in a maroon suit and top hat was on the stairs opening the door for customers and bowing them through. The whole effect was so splendid that Poppy crossed over to the other side of the road in order to view it better. She'd been in one or two imposing buildings before, but always as a servant, through the tradesmen's entrance. Now she was going through the front door wearing an outfit from Harrods and kid-leather gloves.

She reached the end of the road, turned back and crossed to the right side again, hearing three o'clock strike on a distant clock and wondering where to wait. Freddie hadn't said whether they should meet outside the hotel or in it, and she hadn't thought to ask. But if inside, then where exactly? The foyer or the reception desk or the restaurant itself?

For a moment she felt like walking past it again, but she was at the bottom of the stone steps by then and the man in maroon had seen her and bowed. As she climbed the steps, she almost expected him to say, 'Back door for trades, if you don't mind.' Instead he tipped his top hat and said, 'Good afternoon, madam.'

'Good afternoon to you,' Poppy replied sedately.

He opened the door. 'Straight through for Reception, madam.'

Poppy was bowed through into a large area which was thickly carpeted, smelled of lavender and luxury, and contained deeply cushioned sofas and leather chairs. She thanked the doorman, thinking how easy it was, if you were rich, to be charming to people. How pleasant to live this sort of life all the time; the sort of life where coming to the Criterion was an everyday matter and where, here inside the glittering reception area, there didn't even appear to be a war on. Apart from all the people in uniform, of course.

She reached the front desk and looked around. Plenty

of boys in khaki and several Canadians in navy. Lots of glamorous young women either in uniform or in civvy suits which owed something to the military look, with straight, sensible skirts and small, close-fitting hats. But no Freddie, and the clock above the desk now showed just past three o'clock.

He'd forgotten, she decided immediately. And then came a list of other reasons he hadn't appeared: he'd resolved to remain true to Miss Cardew; he was not willing to risk being seen with a housemaid; his mother had forbidden him to come; his unit had been called away on an earlier ship. Or – the most obvious and dreadful thing of all – he had simply stopped caring for her.

'Can I help you, madam?' asked the man behind the desk.

Poppy started. 'Afternoon tea,' she said. 'That is, I am, er . . . meeting a friend for afternoon tea.'

'In Palm Court?'

She nodded, although she had no idea. Was there a choice of places for afternoon tea?

He opened a leather book. 'A three o'clock booking, then. May I ask under whose name?'

'De Vere,' Poppy said after a moment's hesitation. 'Second Lieutenant Frederick de Vere.'

He looked at the book, but gave no indication as to whether he'd found a booking or not and just asked if Poppy would like to go to the table and wait. After another hesitation, wondering which might look less needy – table or Reception – she decided that, yes, she'd go and sit down.

Palm Court was a circular room with a glass roof. The walls were scalloped, each curved shape containing a table for two, while bigger tables surrounded a circular space in the centre, where a woman in a gold evening dress was playing a harp. *A harp!* Poppy had only ever seen a picture of one before, and had somehow imagined that they only existed as mythical instruments played by angels sitting on clouds.

Once seated at a small table with its own softly glowing lamp, Poppy gazed about the room, which was fast filling up with customers. If Freddie didn't arrive, what would she do? Perhaps she could pretend she'd come on her own and order a pot of tea. But how much would it cost? Even a *cup* of tea in a place such as this might possibly be as much as two shillings, and there wasn't much more than that in her purse. But if he didn't come, she thought, then never mind about the cost of tea, because it would break her heart and she'd never get over it! And just after she'd thought *that* – oh joy, there he was, coming across the thickly carpeted floor, smiling at her, and only ten minutes late.

'I thought you weren't coming!' she blurted out, and could have bitten her tongue off for doing so.

'I'm so sorry to be late,' he said. 'Regimental matters, meetings, the tedious checking of mine and the men's equipment – it goes on and on.'

'Oh! Of course it must do. That's quite all right.' She could have forgiven him anything, because he looked handsome, so *very* handsome, that surely every girl there would fall in love with him at first sight. His uniform was newly pressed with no sign of wear nor war, the officer's stripes prominent on his arm. The brass buttons and fixings on his belt glittered, and his hair still flopped over his eyes in an endearing manner.

He sat down and smiled at her. 'You look charming,' he said. 'And that is a very elegant and stylish outfit you're wearing.' He laughed. 'You might think it strange that I know such a thing, but I have two sisters.'

'Of course,' Poppy said. Perhaps you also have Miss Cardew? she couldn't help but think.

'Have you been here before?'

Poppy shook her head. As if she'd ever have dared!

'The menu is very extensive. When my . . . my brother was stationed here before he went to France, my mother came down for tea. She said it was the only place outside France where she could obtain madeleines. She's very fond of madeleines.'

'Is she?' Poppy said politely. She didn't know what these were – and certainly didn't want to be reminded of his mother.

'And so, Poppy Pearson, how are you liking being a nurse?' Freddie asked, settling back in his chair.

'I like it very much,' Poppy said, trying to dismiss thoughts of Mrs de Vere. 'It's very hard work but . . .'

'Better than fighting, given the choice. But you must see a lot of painful sights.'

'We had a boy of only fifteen on our ward until this morning – he'd had his leg shot off and lost a shocking amount of blood.' As she said this she realised that to be talking of such things at the tea table was frightfully ill mannered. 'I'm sorry,' she added quickly. 'It's just that Thomas has been very much on my mind – he's so young and we all made such a pet of him. His mother came down from Newcastle last night and Sister got special permission for the two of them to be escorted by an orderly all the way back to a Newcastle hospital, nearer his home.'

Freddie nodded. 'That should suit him better.'

'Thomas used to have Private Taylor looking out for him, you see, but Taylor's twin was killed by a sniper and since then he's gone downhill and Thomas has gone with him.' She knew she was blabbing but couldn't seem to stop. 'Private Taylor has refused to eat or drink at all now, and Sister's really worried about him.'

There was a pause, then Freddie said, 'You have a brother in the army, don't you? Is he in France?'

Poppy nodded. 'I don't quite know where, though.' She didn't want to think about Billy.

'And what does he think of army life?'

Poppy paused. 'He . . . he's undecided right now,' she said after a moment.

A waitress arrived, pink in the face and eyes ablaze for Freddie (who, Poppy was pleased to see, didn't seem to notice). 'How can I help you, sir? Afternoon tea for two, is it?'

Freddie nodded. 'And two glasses of champagne, please,' he added, much to Poppy's delight, for she had never tasted champagne before.

'At once, sir,' the waitress said, bobbing a little curtsey.

A laden tray soon arrived, carried by a man wearing white gloves. Having spent years serving tea, Poppy was on safe ground, confident about handling the heavy pot and not about to make any mistakes concerning in what order the milk, tea and sugar should go into the cups. The savoury food arrived first: roast beef and crab sandwiches with the crusts cut off, salmon pinwheels, cheese triangles, anchovy puffs, bridge rolls with ham and mustard. There seemed to be no shortages at the Criterion.

Poppy, who'd been too nervous to eat breakfast or lunch, knew that she was starving hungry, but every time she caught Freddie's eye her stomach turned right over and she found herself unable to do much more than nibble at what was before her. In some ways this was a good thing, she thought, because the food looked so delicious compared to what was on offer in the hostel canteen that she might have forgotten her manners and bolted down more than was seemly.

She and Freddie spoke about the tragedy of the *Titanic*, about the possibility of the royal family changing their Germanic-sounding name to one that was more English, and of the case for conscription.

Time passed. Poppy was anxious to ask whether the War Office would inform her if Freddie was injured (for

Mrs de Vere certainly wouldn't), but felt it would sound presumptuous to ask such a thing, as if she was confident that there was a relationship between them. She had high hopes of the champagne making the two of them more relaxed, and drank hers eagerly, but once the bubbles had gone it turned out that there was actually very little in the glass. She certainly didn't feel *squiffy*, as Matthews had assured her she would after drinking alcohol.

Next the scones arrived, luscious, tall as top hats and still warm from the oven. She knew that jam should be put on first then clotted cream, and was managing this quite tidily when she glanced up at one of the larger tables in the centre of the room and, to her horror, saw one of the Netley Hospital matrons, in her full uniform and white winged cap, taking tea with some army officers. She'd only seen this particular lady once, when she'd been on an inspection tour of the wards, and was fairly sure that she wouldn't be recognised in civvies, but it had the effect of making her feel jittery – which in turn re-established the barriers which had gradually been coming down between her and Freddie.

The cakes and sweets came and Poppy changed the angle she was sitting at to be out of the matron's direct sight. Nervously, she took a small chocolate eclair from the cake stand and, biting into it, squirted cream down the front of Jameson's purple jacket. Freddie had to give her his napkin to help mop it up.

Oh, why were things so difficult? Not daring to take another bite from the eclair, she nibbled at a walnut wrapped in marzipan, then, catching Freddie's eye, felt her stomach lurch and put it down again. She felt sick and thought to herself, sick with love. This was all so strange. It was too correct, too proper – they were being much too polite with each other. What she wanted was to be alone with him and to be kissed again, but that was never going to happen here, with someone playing a harp and a matron lurking a few tables away.

She knew she really must say something to him about Miss Cardew – either that or spend the days and weeks to come worrying about her. In her head she rehearsed several beginnings: '*I believe I mentioned in my letter . . .*' and '*Pardon me for asking such a thing . . .*' and even '*Of course, it may not be any of my business . . .*'

In the end, pushing aside a pink macaroon, she blurted out, 'But what about Miss Cardew?'

There was a fraught moment when she thought he was just going to pretend he hadn't heard her, but then he said, '*What* about her?'

Poppy blushed. 'Well, you and she . . . you are . . . at least, what I mean is, are you . . . friends? That is, not friends, but romantically attached?'

Freddie's hand reached for hers across the white linen tablecloth. 'You mustn't worry,' he said. 'Miss Cardew and her family are great friends of my mother and father. The two of us have known each other since we were children.'

'But is there . . . I mean, do you see . . .' Thrown by the way he'd boldly taken hold of her hand in front of the whole restaurant, Poppy came to a stuttering halt.

He gave her hand a squeeze. 'My mother would love there to be a serious attachment between Philippa and me, but . . .'

Poppy never found out what he'd been about to say because the waitress had come up and was standing there smirking at the sight of their two hands joined on the tablecloth. 'Will there be anything else, sir?'

'I think not,' Freddie said. 'Just the bill, please.'

The bill! It was the end of their meeting and she hadn't really found out anything.

The waitress went away and Poppy, not daring to bring up the subject of Miss Cardew again, sat there grasping Freddie's hand, taking in every detail of his face so she could recall it later. *This* was what it was like to be in love, she thought; this was how those weeping girls at the stations felt as they waved their lovers off to fight – a deep distress and a tremendous pride. Freddie was going to save the world!

'Shall we write to each other?' Freddie asked. 'And will you meet me again when I come back through Southampton?'

'Of course!' said Poppy, thinking that she'd have met him at the gates of hell if he'd asked. 'Yes to both things.'

The waitress came up with the bill on a silver tray and Freddie released Poppy's hand, found a pound note in his wallet and paid.

'Thank you for your attention,' he said to the waitress.

'Thank *you*, sir,' she replied, smiling and looking at him from under her lashes. And then as an afterthought added, 'And madam.'

Outside in the street it was growing dark and there was a high wind gusting down the street and making all the ribbons on the bay trees twist and flutter. Poppy had hoped that Freddie would walk back to the hostel with her but, suddenly struck with the notion that they might see someone from the hospital, said she would be perfectly all right on her own; he must go and prepare for his regimental dinner.

Would he kiss her, she wondered. Or maybe he wouldn't think it was right to kiss in the street . . .

While she was still pondering this, they reached the bottom of the hotel steps, just out of view of the doorman, and he put both his hands on her shoulders and kissed the top of her nose.

'Dearest Poppy,' he said. 'The prettiest flower in the field . . .'

The prettiest flower in the field, Poppy repeated to herself dizzily. He *must* love her. She raised her face to his and closed her eyes in preparation for a proper kiss – when there came the sound of running footsteps.

'Poppy!' a voice called. They both turned to see Matthews, puffing and out of breath. 'I didn't know if you'd still be here!'

Poppy stared at her with surprise and a little alarm. 'What is it?'

'I'm so sorry to interrupt, but your ward sister sent a message to the hostel to say that your brother arrived on the last troopship and has been admitted to Netley with a foot injury. You weren't around so the orderly passed the note to me.'

'Billy?' Poppy gasped. 'Is it serious? Is he badly hurt?'

Matthews shook her head. 'She didn't say – just that he'd come in injured and you should go and see him.'

Freddie had already taken his hands from her shoulders. 'Then of course you must go quickly,' he said.

Poppy looked up at him, feeling quite desperate. 'Thank you for a lovely tea. I'm so sorry I have to . . .'

'I'll write to you,' said Freddie.

Then Matthews was taking her arm and hurrying her down the road towards the hospital.

Chapter Nineteen

'I'm so sorry I had to interrupt you,' Matthews said, 'but I thought you'd want to know at once. Just in case he's seriously injured and . . . well, you know.'

'Yes, of course. Thank you. I'm glad you came,' said Poppy in a distracted voice. She glanced behind them to the retreating figure of Freddie. Would he turn and look at her? If he really cared, he would. And yes! As he reached the corner, he turned round and gave her a wave.

'How did it go?' Matthews asked.

'It was blissful,' Poppy said. 'I mean, it was all strange at first, and I felt so nervous I could hardly eat a *thing*, but he held my hand over the table and we just *looked* at each other and whenever we did my stomach turned over. He told me that this other girl I've been worried about is just a family friend and that there's nothing between them.'

'He's very handsome.'

'I know!' Poppy said with a sudden surge of feeling. 'He looks quite divine in his uniform. The waitress couldn't take her eyes off him, and when he took my hand at the table she was absolutely goggling at us.' She sighed, then gave her head a little shake as if to clear it and looked at Matthews with something approaching panic on her face. 'Our Billy, though! How did Sister sound when she told you? How on earth am I going to tell Ma if he . . . if he . . .'

Matthews put her arm around her friend's shoulder. 'Don't let's talk about it until we know more. It may just be a piece of shrapnel or a broken toe or something.'

Poppy shook her head, knowing that Matthews was just trying to make her feel better, for both girls were well aware that minor injuries were dealt with at a field hospital close to the front. 'No, not if he got a Blighty ticket for it.'

At the main reception desk of the hospital, it took quite some time for Private William Pearson to be located, and when the orderly eventually discovered that Poppy's brother was in Hut 600, he gave her a strange look. A concerned yet slightly disdainful look.

'Why did he look at me in that funny way?' Poppy asked Matthews as they made their way across gravel and grass towards the higher number huts at the back of the hospital.

Matthews shook her head. 'I've no idea.'

'He did look at me strangely though, didn't he? Do you think it's the hut assigned to those who are about to . . . about to die?'

'No, of course not,' said Matthews. 'Look, we're nearly there.' As they approached the hut, she asked, 'Are you sure you wouldn't rather be on your own? You can say.'

'No!' Poppy said with some panic. 'Please . . .'

'It's all right,' Matthews said. 'I'm happy to stay with you, I just wanted to make sure I wasn't intruding.' She shone her torch beam on to the hut number. 'Six hundred. This is it.' She flashed the torch across the outside. 'This is much smaller than our huts.'

'And look!' Poppy broke in. 'It's got bars on the windows. Why ever would they want to put bars on the windows?'

Matthews shrugged to say that she didn't know.

'I just hope the night staff will let me see Billy for a moment,' Poppy said, tapping at the door. 'Or at least tell me how he is.'

She had to knock twice more before someone came, and then it wasn't a nurse or an orderly but an armed soldier who came to the door. Seeing him, Poppy sensed that something was seriously wrong and was too taken aback to speak, so Matthews spoke up instead.

'Pearson and I are both VADs here at the hospital,' Matthews said. 'She's heard that her brother's been sent here injured, and she wonders if she could see him or at least find out how he is.'

'Pearson, did you say? First name William?'

'That's right,' Poppy said in a choked voice. She was terribly afraid of hearing something she didn't want to hear – that Billy had died after being admitted or was undergoing a serious operation or wasn't expected to last the night.

'He's got a foot injury – a gunshot wound,' said the soldier. He spoke sharply, matter of factly, not at all like the way Sister and Nurse Gallagher spoke to worried relatives.

'Is it bad?' Poppy faltered. 'Really bad?'

'That's all I can tell you. You'll have to come and enquire in the morning. You can't come in now.'

'But why is he right out here? Is there something different about this ward?' Poppy asked.

The soldier looked at Poppy sardonically. 'You could say that.'

Poppy couldn't frame the next question so it was left to Matthews to ask, 'Can you tell us what?'

'William Pearson is under arrest. He has a self-inflicted wound.'

Poppy stared at him. '*Self-inflicted?*'

'Put it this way, rather than go into battle and fight alongside his pals, he chickened out and shot himself in the foot.'

Poppy swayed against Matthews, who put her arm firmly around her friend and glared at the soldier.

'We'll be back here tomorrow,' Matthews said.

Poppy didn't sleep. Couldn't sleep. How *could* Billy do such a thing? How could he let down his pals and shoot himself like that? What on earth would happen to him?

Sister Kay spoke to her about it when she arrived at Hut 59 the next morning. Taking her to one side, she said with some sympathy, 'I'm afraid it doesn't look good for your brother.'

'How bad is not good?' Poppy asked.

'I believe it depends on whether his company was under fire at the time. If he endangered other men's lives by his actions, then his sentence could be a severe one.' Sister added quietly, 'Pearson, your brother could be facing a death sentence.'

Poppy stared at her, hardly able to take in her words. It was one thing for a boy to die in the service of his country – of course his family would mourn him desperately, but there was a sense that his death was a glorious sacrifice and comfort could be taken from that. But dying as a punishment for cowardice was something very different and terribly shameful.

Poppy had her regular duties to attend to in Hut 59. She did these automatically, hardly responding to the banter from the boys, and it wasn't until after eleven o'clock that Sister could spare her to go across to Hut 600.

There were two armed guards on the door and Poppy had to fill in a form to be admitted. Inside the hut it was bleak – there were no cartoons or posters on the walls, no pictures of music-hall singers cut out of newspapers, no sign of card games, of board games, music or pot plants. There were only three men in the hospital beds and there didn't seem to be any VADs to attend to them, just two burly male orderlies.

Billy was in bed, turned towards the wall, with a cage holding the weight of the blankets from his leg.

'Billy,' Poppy whispered.

The mound of blankets didn't move and Poppy was reminded of the way young Thomas had been.

'Billy!' she hissed again. 'I've only got ten minutes.'

After a moment, Billy turned in the bed, rolled back the blanket and looked at Poppy, misery etched on his face. He looked so pale and desperate that Poppy, who'd had every intention of speaking to him sharply and saying how disappointed she was, burst into tears. He might have behaved badly, but he was family – her little brother.

'Billy!' She put her head down on the bed and wept. 'How *could* you? What will Ma say? It will break her heart.'

Billy cried too then, oblivious of the cold stares of the orderlies. When they'd both done nothing but sob for a minute, Poppy dried her eyes on the edge of her apron.

'I have to go back to my ward soon,' she said, 'but before I do, I want you to tell me how it happened.'

Billy sniffed, wiped his nose on his pyjama sleeve. 'I dunno . . .'

'I need to try and understand. I got your letter and I know what you've been going through, but to shoot yourself like that . . . How could you do such a thing?'

It was a full two minutes before Billy could pull himself together enough to speak, and he did so with a tremor to his voice and many stops and starts. 'It was like I wrote in my letter to you,' he said. 'Guns day an' night, enough to drive you mad, and you couldn't put your head above the parapet or you'd get shot at. An' officers shouting at you, and water in the trenches, an' nowhere to sit or lay your head, an' . . . an' . . .' he paused and gulped, '. . . an' the mates you'd gone out with ending up splayed on the barbed wire like they was target practice for Fritz, or getting a grenade lobbed at them and lying there on the mud with their guts spilling out or their faces half off . . .'

'*Billy!*' Poppy cried in horror, putting up her hand to stop him.

'That's what it was like. My mate Banksey 'ad both feet shot off and left half his stomach out there, and when they dragged him back he took six hours to die.' Billy closed his eyes. 'I could tell you more. I could tell you worse stuff about blokes with their heads blown off an' rats eating their insides, but I don't want you to have nightmares like I do.'

Poppy pressed her lips together, trying to control the wave of nausea sweeping through her body. 'And so you . . . ?'

'So the morning after Banksey died, when I was supposed to climb out of the trench and run towards Fritz with my bayonet, I just couldn't do it. I got out my gun an' . . . and shot myself in the foot and said a sniper had got me. And I'm not sorry I did it. At least I didn't have to face the Jerries.'

'Sshhh,' Poppy said, glancing towards the orderlies. 'But how did the officers find out?'

'The officers bloody know everything, don't they? You'd think amid all the stuff what's going on they wouldn't notice a stray shot, but they did. Anyway, the lieutenant was already watching me – I hadn't exactly been the first up and over the day before. Had the shakes badly, I did, and a blinding headache, and I'd been vomiting.'

'Wasn't that enough to get you off?'

He shook his head. 'They think you're just swinging the lead.'

'And are the other two men in here . . . ?'

He shook his head. 'Dunno. We're not allowed to talk to each other.'

'And what will happen to you all?'

'There'll be a court martial first,' Billy said huskily. 'Then they reckon . . . well, we'll be shot, that's what they reckon. They take you out at dawn and shoot you like a rabbit.'

'No!'

Billy put out a shaking hand and touched hers briefly, but Poppy's shout had attracted the attention of one of the orderlies.

'That's time enough,' he said. 'We don't usually allow visitors in here.'

'Just a minute,' Billy said. He passed her a postcard. 'I've got this to send to Ma, but I haven't told her what's happened.' He shrugged helplessly. 'I don't know what to say. Write what you like and send it.'

Poppy took it, gave Billy's thin, cold body a brief hug, then left him.

Her eyes were filled with tears when she came out of the hut and, going across the soaking wet grass hardly able to see where she was going, she almost collided with a young man in a white jacket.

'Hey, steady!' Michael Archer said. Then added in surprise, 'Ah, it's my friendly nursing VAD.'

Poppy, choking back tears, said, 'I'm awfully sorry, sir. I can't stop.'

But he was holding her elbow. 'Whatever's wrong?' he asked. 'Can I help at all?'

Poppy shook her head. 'It's not me. It's my brother . . .'

'Injured?' He looked at her carefully. 'Worse?'

'Worse. As bad as it could be.'

He frowned, thoughtful. 'But not dead?'

'No. He . . . he's just here.' Seeing no reason to keep the shameful secret from someone who might be treating Billy, she added, 'He's in Hut 600.'

'Ah.'

'I'm afraid he shot himself in the foot.'

Michael Archer shook his head slowly. 'I see. A self-inflicted.'

'But in a way I can understand!' Poppy said quickly. 'He said he hadn't slept at all since his regiment got to France because of the continual gunfire – he was almost demented with it.'

The young doctor nodded sympathetically.

'And he'd seen dreadful sights . . . his mates dying in the most awful circumstances.'

'I can't begin to imagine,' he said. 'I know it's truly, truly dreadful out there.'

There was such sympathy in his voice that Poppy almost began weeping again. 'He'd been suffering terrible headaches and vomiting. I went in there all ready to say how ashamed I was but ended up crying with him.'

'What these boys go through is almost unbearable,' said Michael Archer with a sigh. 'God alone knows how they stick with it.'

'Billy didn't . . .' Poppy said. She realised that Michael Archer was still holding on to her elbow and managed to smile at him. 'Thank you so much for your interest, but forty-six portions of meat pie will have arrived at my ward by now and I must go and serve them.'

'Look, if you like, I'll go and see your brother,' Michael Archer said. 'Talk to him, see if I can do anything to help.'

'Would you?' Poppy's eyes brimmed with tears again. 'Thank you! I'd be so grateful.'

That night, Poppy sat up late, spending some time looking at the field postcard that Billy had given her to send to their mother. It depicted a smiling Tommy giving the thumbs-up sign and was pre-printed so that someone who'd had an injury to their eyes or their hand would still, with a bit of help, be able to tick a box to let their loved ones know they were *wounded slightly*, *wounded seriously* or *coming home*.

Billy had not filled in anything. After some thought Poppy decided that she wouldn't send it, but would write a proper letter instead.

YWCA Hostel,
Southampton

28th October 1915

Dearest Ma,
You must try not to worry about what I'm going to tell you, but I'm writing to let you know that our Billy has been sent home from France and is here in the hospital

with an injury to his foot. I have seen him today and he sends you all his love. The best news is that I know a doctor here who is taking a personal interest in him.

I will write to you again after his foot has been sorted out and persuade him to write to you as well. I think he is very relieved to be home and is in no hurry to return to France. It is pretty terrible out there.

We remain very busy here in Hut 59. As our patients get better and leave to convalesce, new boys join us, and we have been told to expect a big convoy in soon. If you could see me, Ma, racing about behind Sister and Nurse, carrying towering piles of linen, balancing bandages and juggling kidney bowls, you'd be amazed. We are on the go all the time; one of the boys said that when he gets better he's going to the workshop to make me some shoes with wheels on so that I can go faster!

Some nice things happen here too. I went for afternoon tea at a very posh restaurant and had a glass of champagne! But I will tell you all about it another time, for I want to post this letter to you straight away.

I will write again soon, but do try not to worry about Billy. He is in the best place, as we always say.
Fondest love to you all,

Poppy

Chapter Twenty

YWCA Hostel,
Southampton

11th November 1915

Dear Freddie,

I know you are somewhere in France and sometimes try to picture you in your dugout, doing your paperwork by the light of a torch with the constant sound of gunfire. I do think about you a lot and hope that you are keeping safe. I know one shouldn't mention anything about the war for fear of our correspondence being read by the enemy, but I do wish I knew where you were. I would plot your position on a map and try and find out a little about the area, so that I could better picture you in your surroundings.

I am so sorry that I had to rush off the other evening, and my friend Matthews wants to apologise to you as *well. The good news is that my brother does not seem too badly injured. He had a foot injury which has now been set by one of the surgeons here at Netley and I have been able to see him once or twice since then.*

I was very happy to hear that you and Miss Cardew are only friends and I trust you forgive me asking about such a thing. Rumours abound below stairs in a big house and I'm afraid 'the family' upstairs is usually the best topic of gossip! The boys in my ward are the same, always on the lookout for rumours and scandal.

I expect it will be strange for you to go home to Somerset rather than Airey House. I hope your family have settled in well and are quite content there. Freddie, there is another question I wish to ask you and I hope you don't think it too impertinent. Does your mother have any idea that we are seeing each other?

Please do tell me if you are short of anything – I would love to send you a parcel.

Goodnight for now. You are much in my thoughts and I hope to dream of you.
Love always,

Poppy

'Jameson? Are you ready for breakfast?' Poppy called over the curtain early the next morning.

'Almost!' Jameson tugged her curtain open and stood there buttoning on her starched white cuffs. 'These cuffs – such a fiddle! Anyway, half the time you have to take them off to do any proper work . . . Now it's just my collar to go . . .'

Poppy, glancing at the open neck of the other VAD's dress, saw, hanging on a chain, a heavy gold ring. A man's ring with a dark green stone.

'I say, Jameson, that's a lovely ring!' Poppy exclaimed.

To Poppy's surprise, Jameson's cheeks flushed red. 'Yes . . . er, it's my father's,' she said, hurriedly doing up the starched collar and slipping into sturdy shoes. 'Ready! Shall we go?'

'It was definitely a man's ring,' Poppy said to Matthews later, scraping margarine on to thick slices of bread in the hospital canteen. 'But I bet it's not her father's.'

'Gosh,' said Matthews. 'D'you think she's engaged, then? Why wouldn't she say she's been seeing someone?'

Poppy shook her head. 'I'm positive she didn't have that ring when we first came here. I've seen her in a nightdress often enough and never noticed it before.' She looked round the hospital canteen. 'Who do we think gave it to her?'

Matthews sighed. 'I'm afraid there's only one answer.'

'Exactly,' Poppy said. 'Her German!'

'She's going to get in terrible trouble.'

'She is.'

The girls spread jam on their bread and Matthews continued, 'Because although he may be the nicest chap in the world and love Jameson to pieces, he's going to want Germany to win the war.'

'Of course,' Poppy said.

They didn't speak any more about Jameson, and as they were leaving the canteen Matthews asked if Poppy had any more news of her brother.

She shook her head. 'They're not keen on letting me into the ward. Billy's foot has been set, apparently, and now I'm waiting to hear how he is from my doctor friend. He said he'd keep me up to date.'

Matthews looked at her mischievously. 'Oh, your *doctor friend* . . . ?'

'It's not like that!' Poppy said. 'My heart belongs to Freddie.'

'Then fingers crossed that *his* heart belongs to you.'

That day the afternoon post for Hut 59 brought a letter which Sister Kay read to them.

> *Downleigh Convalescent Home,*
> *Purbridge, Newcastle*
>
> *18th November 1915*
>
> *Dear Sister-in-charge,*
> *I am writing on behalf of Thomas Stilgoe, who has lately been under your esteemed care in Netley Hospital.*
> *Thomas is making good progress and his leg is healing*

well. He is very glad to be back among his people and his mother comes in most days to see him. Thomas will not be going back into the army, of course, being only fifteen. He has received a wound stripe to wear on his demob suit, and is very proud of it.

I am writing with what might seem a trivial thing but is most important to Thomas. He was keeping safe what he calls his 'lucky charm', a shard of shrapnel which the doctors removed from the back of his neck and which, he was told, had it been half an inch closer, would have penetrated his brain. Apparently he kept this in his locker in Hut 59, but in the rush and trouble of leaving, he forgot to take it. He worries me day and night about it, and I wondered if there is a slim chance that it might have dropped on to the floor somewhere?

I appreciate that being in the principal hospital and caring for the very large numbers of men straight from the front must be difficult in the extreme, and on behalf of the nursing staff in all corners of Britain, thank you for your untiring work.

I remain, yours respectfully,

Edna Plumridge
Matron

'Well,' Sister said after reading out the letter, 'I am perfectly sure that it is *not* on the floor somewhere and I'm rather irritated that she could even suggest such a thing. Does she think we don't sweep floors in Southampton?'

'But she did thank us very nicely,' said Nurse Gallagher.

'Hmm,' said Sister. 'Pearson, when you've taken back the tea things, would you have a look around Thomas's locker?'

'Yes, of course,' Poppy said, and glanced over to what had been Thomas's bed. Then she noticed something. 'Private Taylor! Where's he gone?'

'Ah.' Sister Kay shook her head sadly. 'As you know, he's been very low, and last night a doctor diagnosed pneumonia and had him moved to a medical ward. They'll let us know how he's getting on.' She shook her head. 'I'm afraid I'm not very hopeful, though. It seems the poor chap just doesn't want to live without his brother.'

Poppy, sighing a little at this news, took the tea things into the kitchen, where a new innovation for the hospital, a domestic VAD, was standing by. Spared the washing-up, Poppy went to have a look around and about Thomas's bed. She knew how superstitious the boys were about the little pieces of shrapnel that had been removed from their bodies, preserving them carefully to send either to their girlfriends as a token of how close they'd been to death, or to keep for themselves as lucky touchstones. If a precious piece of shrapnel got lost under the bed or happened to be tidied away before visiting time, then there was no rest for whoever was on duty until it was found again.

The new occupant of Thomas's bed, a nineteen-year-old named Albert Leeway, seemed to be asleep, for the top sheet had been pulled right up over his face.

'Excuse me, Private Leeway,' Poppy said, and she twitched at the sheet to alert him to the fact that she was there.

The sheet slipped back and revealed a bright red balloon with a clown's face painted on it. Poppy gave a scream – she couldn't help herself – and from the rest of the ward came guffaws of laughter.

'Sorry, nurse,' said Private Mackay when he stopped laughing. 'My wife sent me a packet of balloons to do up the ward for Christmas and the boys have been itching to play a trick on you.'

Poppy fanned herself. 'You lot are absolute rotters!' she said as the real Private Leeway appeared round a screen.

'But, nurse, we're harmless!' called Private Mackay. Then there was a strange and rather awful hiatus while everyone realised what he'd said and didn't know whether to laugh. 'I suppose I should say *armless*,' continued Private Mackay in a stunned voice.

Poppy, looking at him, wanted to go and hug him, but knew the hospital authorities wouldn't think it appropriate.

To everyone's satisfaction, she found the missing piece of shrapnel in the back of the locker and this was sent off to Thomas. Sister wrote a covering letter to his matron, while the rest of the ward called out the various messages and good wishes they wanted conveyed to him. It was quite true, Poppy thought as she listened to them: the boys of Hut 59 could be absolute rotters, but she absolutely loved every one of them.

It was nearly eight o'clock before she left the hospital that evening and, going out through the gates, met Michael Archer coming in.

'I'm so pleased to see you!' she said. And when he gave her his beaming smile, added quickly, 'Oh, I don't mean in that way!' in case he got the wrong idea. Then, thinking that sounded too blunt, murmured, 'I mean, it is always nice to see you, but . . .'

'That's all right,' he interrupted, putting down his heavy leather bag. 'I'd like to think that you want to see me for myself alone . . .' here he put his hand on his heart, '. . . but I know it's because of your brother.'

Poppy smiled. 'I'm just so grateful to have you looking out for him.'

'Well, to start with, the operation on his foot seems to have been a success. Luckily there wasn't much damage to the small bones of the ankle.'

'That's grand.'

'As to the other matter – the more serious matter concerning his crime – have you ever heard of shell shock?'

Poppy shook her head.

'It's a new name for what they used to call *nerves*. I'm afraid it's an increasing problem with men who've been under fire, a nervous debility which can manifest itself as acute fear of noise, unpredictable behaviour, sickness, dread.'

'Billy spoke about all those things.'

Michael Archer nodded. 'I'm no specialist in that particular field, but it seems to me that your brother is suffering from this shell shock and, once he's recovered from surgery, should have proper psychiatric help.'

'And what does that mean, exactly?' Poppy asked, wondering if her brother was mad.

'It means that his shell shock might be considered an illness, and his shooting himself a symptom of that illness.' On Poppy frowning, he added, 'Well, think of it: a boy living a sheltered life at home with his doting mother is taken to an alien place where people are attempting to kill him. He's deprived of sleep and comforts, he sees his friends dying in more and more gruesome ways . . . Who could blame him for wanting to get out of it? He must have been almost mad with terror.'

Poppy nodded slowly.

'We have officers – highly educated men, authors and poets – in our psychiatric unit whose fear has manifested itself in all sorts of bizarre ways. If officers can be found to be suffering from nerves, I see no reason why a regular Tommy shouldn't. When you think of it, a man has got to be a little mad to dare to inflict such tremendous pain on himself.'

'Really?' Poppy asked, her heart lifting a little. 'So there might be a reason for Billy's behaviour and he might not be . . . condemned to death?'

He nodded. 'A number of enlightened doctors are saying that a man shouldn't be called a traitor just because he's terrified. I'm going to recommend that, while your brother's foot is healing, he be sent to a hospital for nervous diseases.'

'And not court-martialled?'

'Not if I can help it.'

Poppy closed her eyes briefly, fighting back tears. 'I'm so grateful, sir. I don't know how to thank you.'

'It's Michael,' he said, picking up his case. 'And, please – I'm only doing my job.'

'Well, thank you for doing it! Thanks awfully,' Poppy said. He was such a jolly nice chap . . .

Chapter Twenty-One

A few days later Poppy, Matthews and Jameson were having breakfast together in the hostel canteen. While Jameson read out requests in the newspapers that the public put their savings into war bonds, Poppy looked at the pages containing the names of the latest casualties to make sure that there were no de Veres amongst them. Having satisfied herself that Freddie wasn't on the *Died in Action* or *Died of Injuries Received* lists, she counted up the days since she'd written to him.

It had been eight days. *Eight days!* Surely he should have replied by now? At the start of the war the post office had said that letters to and from those on active service would be delivered as soon as possible, within two or three days. This meant, she calculated on her fingers, that if Freddie had written back as soon as he'd received her letter, she should have heard four days ago. But perhaps he wasn't going to write back! Perhaps he thought she had no business asking if his mother knew about their relationship. Perhaps he thought the way she'd signed off, *love always*, was a bit too much.

'Might my signing off like that have frightened him off?' she asked Matthews.

'Of course not!' Matthews protested. 'Give the chap a chance – eight days is nothing. He probably hasn't even received your letter yet. Besides, a soldier has other things on his mind besides writing to his sweetheart.'

'He's probably up to his neck in mud and bullets,' said Jameson.

'I read somewhere that sixteen thousand mailbags go off to France every day,' Matthews said. 'Your letter is just a tiny drop in a huge ocean.'

Poppy nodded. 'All right.' She heaved a sigh. 'I'll try not to mention it again.'

'You can try,' Matthews said, grinning, 'but I rather think you *will* mention it . . .'

'Oh, look!' said Jameson, who'd been reading a list of those who had *Died of Injuries Received*. 'There was a memorial service in London yesterday for a German officer who was a British prisoner of war.'

Poppy and Matthews looked at her.

'So?' Matthews asked rather sternly.

'Well, nothing really. I'm just telling you what it says,' said Jameson. And she read out: *'British officers paid their respects and laid a wreath on the bier of Major Christian von Statten, taken prisoner at Ypres, who died of his wounds in Westminster Hospital.'* She looked at them earnestly. 'I mean, the very fact that high-up British officers attended

his funeral goes to show that they held him in respect.'
When the other two girls didn't comment on this, she
added, 'Look, when it comes down to it, every soldier,
British or German, is just fighting to protect his country,
isn't he? How could anyone be blamed for doing that?'

Matthews got up abruptly to take their dishes back.

'Honestly, Jameson, I don't think you should be working on that ward any longer,' Poppy said. 'You're going to
get yourself into trouble.'

'I don't know what you mean,' Jameson said, and
returned to her newspaper.

Poppy made up her mind to ask Sister's advice about
the matter, using a different name and situation, but
going into the ward that morning she saw there wasn't
going to be the opportunity. Astonishingly, the night
staff were still on duty, everything was topsy-turvy and a
convoy of badly wounded soldiers was expected in at any
time. Bed space was desperately needed, so, to accom-
modate newcomers, those patients from Hut 59 and
other wards who were due to be moved to convalescent
homes had been given their blue hospital suits (winter
warm, lined with flannelette) and were now temporarily
'camping out' on canvas chairs in the long airy corridors
of the main hospital.

'Oh, thank heavens for another VAD!' the night
nurses greeted her.

Poppy was kept busy for the rest of the morning
scrubbing down old lockers ready for the new men,
requisitioning sheets and blankets from the linen store,

airing mattresses with hot water bottles and making up beds precisely as Sister Kay liked them.

By eleven o'clock everything was ready. The newly vacated beds had been made up with crisp sheets and clean counterpanes and each had its top sheet folded back invitingly. A new pair of pyjamas, vest and hand-knitted bedsocks waited on each pillow and there was a white enamel bowl on every locker, containing a soap and flannel, toothbrush, razor and comb. The incomers probably would not be bothered with washing and shaving for a day or more, but when they did, they would find everything they needed.

By midday, though, the staff of Hut 59 were still waiting for their convoy and the night nurses had gone home to get some sleep. Poppy took the dinner trays round, then cleared them away and did the washing-up, helped by two 'up patients' who, keen to see the new boys and have news from the front, had volunteered to give her a hand.

After dinner, Poppy was asked to go and see how Private Taylor was doing in the ward for pneumonia cases, and discovered that medical wards were very different from surgical wards, mainly because all the patients in these huts were very gravely ill. It was considered important that they had as much fresh air as possible, so the ward's large windows were permanently open to the sea breezes. Despite this health-restoring wind, however, most of the patients were comatose, so the only sound in there was of the wind buffeting outside and the dry rasping of men struggling to breathe. There was none of the banter that Poppy had come to expect on the surgical wards, no singing, no gossip nor plaintive calls of 'Nurse! Can you come and tuck me up!'

'I've come to enquire about Private Taylor,' Poppy said to the nurse sitting at the front desk.

'Private Taylor . . .' The nurse sighed and shook her head. 'He's not at all well, I'm afraid. Do you know him personally?'

'Well, I'm a VAD from his last ward. Sister sent me.'

The other girl shrugged. 'He's a tragic case.'

'I know. His twin . . .'

'Yes.' The girl looked at Poppy sadly. 'We've sent for his people. All I can say is, we're doing our best.'

At two o'clock a message came from the docks to say that, owing to rough weather, the hospital ship had only just managed to drop anchor beside the pier, and as a consequence as many hands as possible were needed to help get the injured men off safely before the tide turned. Hearing this, Sister asked Poppy, Moffat and Smithers to go down to the docks, saying she and Nurse Gallagher would stay at Netley to begin the nursing care of the incoming soldiers as soon as they arrived.

'Do whatever you can,' she told them both. 'You may find yourselves mopping up sick – or worse, if there are dysentery cases on board – sluicing down decks, holding the hand of a man who's dying or escorting a blinded man on to a train. Whatever you do, and however ghastly the sight before you, please try to carry out your duties willingly and conscientiously. And *smile*,' she added. 'After all they've been through, those boys deserve a smile.'

Poppy, Moffat and Smithers joined the bus-loads of VADs and orderlies going down to the quayside. For some, it was their first important outing as VADs; for others it was something they'd undertaken before. Everyone was quiet and solemn, and if they spoke to each other it was in whispers. They were uneasy because of the scale of the operation: there were hundreds – possibly thousands – of injured men coming home, so were these numbers an indication of how the war was going? Were there as many casualties on the German side? They wondered and surmised, but kept their notions to themselves. It was not patriotic to have doubts.

Poppy was awe-struck at the sight of the hospital ship. It was a dull day and the sky was ashen, but the ship, now safely moored, was painted glossy white and, with lights glowing along its walkways and portholes, shone like a giant lantern in the gloom. On the sides of the ship huge red crosses were painted, indicating that it carried injured men only, and should be allowed to sail unimpeded to and from the French and English ports.

Along the dock were lines of lorries, carts, charabancs and private cars waiting to convey the weary patients to Southampton hospitals or the station and then, if they were considered well enough to stand the journey, on to other hospitals in other cities.

The bus carrying Poppy and the others got as close to the ship as possible. There were, Poppy saw, two gang-planks from ship to shore and VADs, doctors, nurses and orderlies were streaming up one of them and coming back down the other, pushing wheelchairs, supporting boys on crutches, carrying stretchers or helping along limping or hopping soldiers, some of whom were trailing bloodied bandages.

Once they were all on board, the VADs and orderlies from Netley stood on the deck waiting to be told where to go and what they should do first.

Poppy, apprehensive about what she might see, clutched at Moffat's arm. 'The *smell*,' she whispered, for the combined stench of overflowing latrines, dried blood, gangrenous wounds and sea-sickness was ghastly in the extreme.

'Awful.' Moffat nodded. 'Try not to breathe in too deeply.'

An army doctor addressed them, his voice hoarse with tiredness. He had blood all down his jacket, Poppy noticed, and his hands were stained with iodine.

'We've been able to do a very quick assessment of most of the men on the way over,' he began. 'The majority are now labelled with the type of injury they have so that they can be sorted on to trains more easily. Don't touch anyone with a red stripe on their label.'

'Why's that?' Poppy asked.

'These are men with dangerous head wounds, those liable to haemorrhages and convulsions, or those who may need emergency treatment at any moment,' said the army officer. 'They must only be moved by a doctor. Some of these boys have come straight from the field and are in a very bad way.'

'How do we know who to take first?' someone asked.

'Take whoever you come to,' came the reply. 'Some of these young men shouldn't have travelled at all, but there was no more room in France. Just let's get these boys off!'

The Netley VADs were shown into what had once been, in the heady days before the war, the luxury cruise ship's dining salon. Crystal chandeliers still swung overhead and the turquoise walls were painted with a lavish underwater scene, but where there had once been linen-clad tables, silver cutlery and sparkling glasses, now there was nothing but rows and rows of makeshift beds, each containing an injured man. *Dreadfully* injured, Poppy thought, looking about her and seeing blood and dirt, torn uniforms, stained bandages, gaping wounds and caked-on mud. In the rush to get them away, some of the men had come straight from battlefield to ship, and had not had even the most rudimentary of clean-ups or any dressing of their wounds.

Poppy stood in the midst of this horror, her heart aching, hardly able to believe what she was seeing. So many men; such ghastly injuries . . .

'All these men must be taken off the ship before the tide turns,' said the army officer. 'The doctors at the foot of the gangplank will read their labels, make a decision about where to send them and list their names so we know where to find them again. If the patient is unconscious or doesn't seem to know who he is, then look for his tag to give his name to whoever is taking details.'

'What if he can't speak and his tag's gone?' someone asked.

The officer spread his hands as if to say he had no idea. 'Just try and find some distinguishing mark. Look at his cap badge for his regiment perhaps.' He indicated the salon. 'Ladies and gentlemen, your patients are waiting.'

Poppy took a deep breath, forced a smile and went in.

By five o'clock, most of the casualties had been taken off the ship. Private George Williams hadn't been left until last deliberately, but his wounds were so terrible and – as much to spare his own feelings as anything else – his stretcher had been placed behind a pillar. Private Williams had taken a grenade hit and one of his arms was no longer there, but it was his face that had come off the worst. Someone had pulled what remained of his khaki jacket collar up as high as possible, but the mess that had once been his face was still clearly visible.

Coming across him suddenly, Poppy didn't have time to compose herself or make his face a little out of focus, and couldn't help but give a small gasp of shock. 'Oh, I didn't know anyone was behind this pillar!' was all she could say to cover herself.

There came a strange, choked reply, for Private Williams couldn't speak: most of his mouth and a good deal of the right side of his jaw were missing. The hole where it had been was now plugged with muslin, but this must have been done some time ago, for the material was dark and dried, and smelled like rotten meat.

Fighting down a wave of nausea, Poppy bent over and looked at his label. She must keep talking, she thought – talking and smiling.

'Hello, Private Williams. You've a smashed arm? We have lots of men with limbs missing on my ward – that is, Hut 59.' She stretched her mouth upward in what she hoped looked like a smile and not a grimace. 'Maybe you'll be coming to us. Sister Kay is *very* nice. You're assured of a warm welcome from her and Nurse Gallagher.'

As she straightened up, the man's eyes followed her.

'Will you be able to walk off the ship with my help?' She smiled again. Too much smiling, she thought, but it was either that or scream. 'Would you prefer a stretcher or a wheelchair? Maybe a stretcher would be better, in case your legs are wobbly.' She smiled again – smiled until her face began to ache. She was asking all these questions, but how was he going to answer her?

He tapped the pocket of his torn, blood-stained jacket. Poppy felt inside, then drew out a pencil and small notepad.

'Ah! Of course,' she said.

She held the notepad on his chest, placed the pencil in his hand and he laboriously printed the words *On stretcher. Please cover face.*

There was a long moment during which she re-read his words several times and struggled to find the right reply. 'I understand what you mean,' she said finally. 'I'll go and get an orderly, a stretcher and a covering.' She blinked back a sudden rush of tears. 'I'm so sorry, you must excuse me. I've seen so many men today . . .'

Please cover face.

Sometimes she felt she couldn't bear another moment of this war.

Chapter Twenty-Two

As fate would have it, Private George Williams was indeed one of the eight 'new boys' assigned to Hut 59. Poppy felt that she'd half-known this was going to happen: that her ward would get him. Somehow a higher power had placed him there so that she could try and make up for her reaction on the troop train.

Tragically, two of Hut 59's new boys were so badly injured that they died within twenty-four hours, and the ward became unusually solemn as two Union-Jack-draped coffins were carried out to the mortuary. The six other Tommies – Private Williams amongst them – lived on.

Talking about the deaths with Moffat in the ward kitchen one morning, Poppy wondered if Private Williams might want to die, too.

'Because what in the world will he do with himself now?' she said, her voice taut with anguish. 'How will he manage with only half a face? He can't eat or talk to anyone, he can't go for a stroll around the grounds. All he does is sit in bed all day hidden behind a newspaper.'

'His face can be reconstructed, though, and we're helping with his eating,' Moffat said, for a device had been made for those patients whose injuries prevented them from taking food or drink in the normal way: a jug and rubber tube affair which sent milk or soup directly down their throats. It took an age to feed a patient in this way, and they hated it, gagging and coughing throughout, but it was either that or they would starve to death.

There was one piece of good news in the hectic and difficult days following the arrival of the Red Cross ship: a message arrived from Private Taylor's ward to say that since his mother had moved to a guest house nearby, he'd begun to eat again, and his prospects seemed brighter.

Billy's leg injury was, as Doctor Archer had predicted, relatively straightforward and the fracture seemed to be healing well in its plaster cast. Two weeks after his operation, Poppy received a note from him saying he was going to be moved to a different hospital and the guards were allowing her to come and see him.

In pelting rain, going across the grass to Hut 600, Poppy could not help feeling relief that Billy was being transferred elsewhere. She'd only visited him two or three times, but had found the visits utterly depressing.

He didn't seem to feel guilty about letting down his mates nor particularly grateful for Doctor Archer's attempts to help him. His attitude was all wrong, Poppy thought.

There was a new inmate in Hut 600 by then, a young man who, Billy told Poppy, had thrown himself on the mud and pretended to be dead when given the command to run with his bayonet towards the German line.

'I told him I didn't blame him one bit,' Billy added.

'Hush,' Poppy said, looking around for the guards. 'You mustn't say things like that – there could be repercussions. It's as if you're encouraging him not to fight.'

'That's just what I am doing.'

'But it's not patriotic.'

'Nor is getting your stomach sliced open by Fritz.'

There were changes in him, though. Poppy noticed that Billy had a twitch above his left eyelid. And his hands, resting on top of the bed, were constantly scratching at the blanket.

'Billy, I can't stay long,' she said. 'Tell me about where you're going.'

'Bloody Scotland,' Billy said.

'Scotland?' Poppy echoed, surprised.

'Your doctor mate came round and told me. I'm going to an asylum for boys who're off their heads.'

Poppy frowned. 'I'm sure he didn't say that. It must be a hospital for nervous diseases.'

'Same thing.'

His nails were chewed right down, Poppy noticed. He hadn't bitten them since he was five!

'It's for those who are suffering from their nerves,' she said. 'Men who've been under fire and who are over-anxious and distressed.'

'You know what everyone calls the place? Dottyville.'

'Better to be in Dottyville than to be dead!' said Poppy, exasperated. 'You don't seem to realise what you've done, Billy – how you've let everyone down.'

'I've heard they give you electric shock treatment there and dunk you in cold water.'

'Stop it!' Poppy said. 'Whatever they do, at least you'll be alive. You're not being shot at dawn, are you?'

'No.' For a brief moment Billy looked scared and younger than his years. 'A loony bin, though! It strikes me that you're all bloody lunatics and I'm the only sane one.'

'Oh, hush! Look, have you written to Ma yet?'

Billy shook his head.

'Well, you must. Tell her you're going to Scotland. You needn't say exactly where, just tell her it's to convalesce or something. And, Billy . . .' she glanced around to make sure no guards were close enough to overhear, 'when you get to this special hospital, don't forget that it's for soldiers affected by their nerves. *Shell shock*, they call it.'

'Yeah. Shell shock,' Billy repeated.

'Try and act a bit vacant and a bit strange, because if they think there's nothing wrong with you, they might still charge you with cowardice under fire.'

Billy shrugged, looking as if he didn't care one way or the other. 'Bloody war . . .'

Two more days went by and Poppy, adding them up, made it fifteen days since she'd written to Freddie. Fifteen days! He'd either decided not to reply to her, or he'd been injured and lost the use of his hands. She wouldn't contemplate the other option.

Coming home late from work on the sixteenth day, however, there was a letter from him waiting for her. Immediately seized with all manner of hopes and fears, she carried it off into the bathroom to be alone with it.

Duke of Greystock's Rgt.

27ᵗʰ November 1915

Dearest Poppy,
Please don't apologise for the swift end to our evening –
of course you had to go and see your brother. I am glad to
hear that his injuries were not serious and hope that he
will be able to return to duty soon.

The sailing over here was quite calm; I believe we were
lucky. When we arrived in Boulogne the Red Cross had
provided tents for the men, showers and a makeshift
canteen, and we made full use of all these until our troop
train turned up. Of course, I am not allowed to divulge
exactly where we are now, but it's not far from the action.

At the moment my unit is in a dugout. We will be moving towards the front if and when we get the command to do so. We are just sitting around waiting, writing letters, reading, carving whistles from wood or playing cards. There are even men who are knitting their own socks. These pastimes may make our life sound rather relaxing, but take my word that it is anything but. There is spasmodic shelling from above, the continual boom of bombs and the ever-present fear of snipers' bullets. To add to this, it has not ceased raining since we arrived and everything we see, touch or do is sodden and muddy.

Poppy, our last meeting was so rushed . . . but I really do want to explain about Miss Cardew. My mother and her very dear friend, Mrs Edna Cardew, have long held the wish that Philippa and I should marry – it was one of those things that were decided when we were in our cradles. I must admit, I was content to go along with things until, as it says in the song, I was smitten by your charms. Since my brother died, Mother has become more insistent that this marriage should take place, and in view of our family tragedy, I have not wanted to upset her. I'm sure you will understand this. However, I have three days' leave in the new year and I intend to speak to my mother very plainly then and tell her that I have no intention of marrying Miss Cardew.

I hope this reassures you. My dear girl, I think of you often and believe we will have our time soon. After I have seen my family, I will be going back to see action via

Southampton and hope we can meet up again. Would
you be able to take a day's leave and we can spend longer
in each other's company?
With fondest regards,

Freddie

The next morning, Poppy read to Matthews the piece
about Freddie's mother and her long-held wishes.

'What do you think?' Poppy asked anxiously. 'It's obvious that no one knows he's seeing me.'

Matthews pulled a face. 'Well . . .'

'It's good that he considers his mother's feelings, of
course.'

'On the other hand, he says he's going to tell her that
he has no intention of marrying Miss Whatsername,
but doesn't say he's going to tell her about you.'

Poppy had noticed this, but was pretending that she
hadn't. 'But look – see here,' she said, holding the letter
in front of her friend's face. 'He says he was smitten by
my charms. And he thinks our time will come!'

'Yes, I know,' Matthews said. 'I suggest you write back,'
she went on, 'but not immediately. Try and keep him guess-
ing a little. You don't want to look too eager.'

'I suppose not.' But she was eager, Poppy thought. She
was . . .

Poppy travelled to the hospital with Jameson that
morning and told her a little about the contents of
Freddie's letter, hoping that she might learn more about

the upper classes and their habit of arranging marriages between their offspring. Jameson was strangely subdued, however, and hardly seemed to take in what Poppy was saying. After a while Poppy stopped talking. There she was, unburdening her heart, and Jameson wasn't even listening!

In Hut 59 that morning, Private Williams's bed, as usual, had two screens around it, as much for his comfort as for anything else. At visiting time or when there were strangers expected on the ward, the screens would be closed so that he was completely hidden from view. The rest of the time there was a narrow gap left between screens, and all the staff, from Sister down to the orderlies, made it a point of honour to go and speak to him at least once in the morning and once in the evening. His face looked just as horrific, but his wounds were cleaned and dressed each morning, and he was as comfortable as any man in his condition could be.

Poppy, doing the rounds with the breakfast trays, wished Private Williams a good morning, then left one of the orderlies to feed him. When she'd washed up the breakfast things, Sister beckoned her over.

'Two jobs for you, Pearson. The first is to take Private Williams to Facial Reconstruction.'

Poppy's heart sank. She was managing as well as she could with the injured soldier, speaking to him brightly and cheerfully and never without a smile, but the thought of taking him somewhere and being with him for any length of time was not an appealing one.

'I know,' said Sister Kay, though Poppy hadn't articulated this, 'but we must try and get him back into society. FR can do great things. They need to assess his face now, early on, before it starts healing.'

'They can't make a whole new face for him, though, can they?'

'Not quite that,' Sister said. 'But they're getting awfully good. The surgeon wants to see him this morning to give him some hope.'

'I'll take him now,' Poppy said, trying to look keen. 'And what's the other thing?'

'Well, I daresay you'll like this better,' Sister said. 'Christmas is coming and last year we didn't do much because we all expected the war to be over. This year we know better, so I want to make Christmas as good as possible for the boys. I'd like you to start collecting bits and pieces for their Christmas stockings.'

Poppy laughed, surprised. 'Oh, yes please!'

'Charities are excellent at donating things, and the big local stores, and tobacco companies and breweries. I'll give you a list.' She hesitated. 'Now, Christmas Day is going to be a day like any other as far as the sick and injured are concerned, so I'm hoping all my staff will be in here that day – that is, if they've nowhere else they ought to be.'

Poppy thought of her ma and sisters far away at Christmas, of Billy in Scotland, of Freddie with his family. 'Nowhere else at all, Sister. I'd like to be on duty.'

'Excellent, Pearson.'

Private Williams had already been told he was going to Facial Reconstruction and an orderly had settled him into a wheelchair. He had a great woolly muffler wound around his neck and, because this completely hid the lower half of his face, to the rest of the world he appeared quite normal. The boys in the ward looked at him, did a double take and, because his mutilated face was hidden, forgot to be awkwardly tactful and spoke to him as if he was no different from anyone else.

'Enjoy your trip to the tin noses shop, Williams!' one shouted.

'Mind you get a corker!'

'Say you want to look like Rudolph Valentino,' called another.

Private Williams could not reply in words, but Poppy felt he was enjoying the change. Either way, he raised his good arm in farewell to his fellow Tommies as she wheeled him from the ward.

Chapter Twenty-Three

YWCA Hostel,
Southampton

1st December 1915

Dear Freddie,
I was very happy to receive your letter! Thank you for letting me know more about Miss Cardew. Your mother only wants your happiness, but surely she will come round to what you want in the end?

I often think of missed opportunities when we were both in Airey House and wonder how these things start. I remember there was a look between us and a smile, but what made that particular look different from all the others, so that we both knew something strange had happened?

Our time will come . . . I treasure those words and try

to imagine where you were and how you felt when you wrote them. To me they foretell a magical time when the war will be over and everything has returned to the way it should be. You are a very long way from here, somewhere unknown, but in Southampton we can sometimes hear the distant thunder of bombs exploding and I shake a little inside when I hear them, for I always fear that they are falling near you.

I would dearly love to see you when you come back through Southampton. How fortunate that I'm working here! I could so easily have been sent to nurse in Birmingham or Liverpool and then we would never be able to meet.

Freddie, I am about to go down to breakfast, so will finish now, hoping that this letter finds you safe.

You are in my heart and in my thoughts.

Poppy xxx

Poppy read through the letter twice, wondering if she'd been too syrupy and sentimental, then in a sudden understanding that it contained the truth – this was how she felt – put the sheets of paper in an envelope and went down to breakfast with Matthews. Jameson came down too, for it was her day off and she'd got up early in order to make the most of it.

'Guess where I went yesterday?' Poppy asked and, after they'd had several fruitless guesses, told them it was the facial reconstruction unit.

'Gosh, what was it like?' Matthews asked. 'Was it gruesome? Like a waxworks?'

Poppy shook her head. 'More like an artist's studio, with photographs pinned all around the room of the men as they were before they were injured, plaster casts of faces on shelves, and baskets containing spectacles and wigs and so on.'

'But how do they make artificial faces?' Jameson asked.

'Well, first of all, any dental work is done – sometimes a new jaw has to be made,' Poppy began. 'After that, the surgeon puts plaster of Paris on to the good portion of a man's face and makes half a mask, and then that gets reversed and stuck to its other half.'

The two girls were looking at her with interest.

'But where does the tin come in?' Matthews wanted to know.

Poppy frowned a little. 'Well, somehow, somewhere along the way, the mask gets transferred – beaten – on to very thin metal.'

'What, and made skin colour?' Matthews said.

Poppy nodded.

'But does the finished article look any good?' said Jameson.

'Does it look *real*?' asked Matthews.

'Well . . .' Poppy hesitated, 'from what I could see of the ones being made, they don't look great, but with a false moustache, or beard and glasses, they're passable. Better than what was there before, at any rate.'

'And have they started making your chap's face yet?' Matthews asked.

Poppy shook her head. 'It's too early. He's got to have dentistry work done on his left side – a new jaw and a new set of teeth. The surgeon wanted to show him what was possible, though, just to cheer him up a bit.'

'And was he cheered?' Matthews asked.

Poppy shrugged. 'I don't think so,' she said. 'Not really.'

'He must be relieved they can do *something*,' Matthews said. 'After all, a person can manage without a leg or arm, but how can they manage without a face?'

They were all quiet for a moment, thinking about this, then Poppy said, 'Private Williams has got to write to his wife and ask her for some photographs of what he looked like before he got hit.'

'Does she know what's happened to him?' Matthews asked.

'I'm not sure,' said Poppy. 'He told me – well, when I say he *told* me . . .' the others nodded to say that they understood and she carried on, '. . . that he'd sent her a field postcard telling her he was being shipped home, but I don't know what he said.'

'What about your Fritz?' Matthews asked Jameson suddenly. 'Is he allowed to send postcards home?'

Jameson, startled, looked at the other two girls as though she'd been cornered. 'What? Why do you ask?' she blustered.

'No particular reason,' Matthews said. 'I just wondered how he kept in touch with his family in Germany.'

247

Jameson looked at them – a sudden, desperate look – then covered her face with her hands.

'Jameson . . .' Poppy said, trying and failing to remember her friend's first name. 'What on earth's the matter?'

Jameson didn't reply, but just shook her head.

Matthews said, 'Is this something to do with your German friend?'

Jameson nodded. 'Reinhart,' she said, in a muffled voice.

'Have you become engaged to him?' Poppy asked, giving Matthews a look of horror.

'Kind of. He's given me his ring.' A long moment went by and then she took her hands away from her face and said. 'But it's not that.'

'What, then?' asked Poppy.

'It's . . . it's all gone wrong.'

'What d'you mean?'

'Well, you see, yesterday . . . yesterday he asked me if I could find out how many hospital ships are docking here, and where most of the casualties are coming from.'

Poppy and Matthews both gasped.

'He wanted you to find out *that*?' cried Poppy.

'He's asking you to spy for him!'

'I know,' said Jameson, not looking at them.

'The absolute scoundrel!' Matthews said in a fierce whisper.

Poppy looked at Jameson sternly. 'I hope you haven't . . .'

248

'Of course I haven't! I wouldn't dream of it! Never!' Jameson got out her handkerchief and blew her nose. 'He was so very nice to me, you see – had such lovely manners and was grateful for everything I did. And then he gave me his ring and asked me to wait for him until after the war.' Jameson wiped her eyes. 'But now I don't know if he ever really cared for me or was just trying to get information.'

'I think possibly the second,' said Matthews drily.

'He may have liked you as well,' Poppy added, feeling sorry for the girl.

'What should I do?' Jameson said pathetically. 'I've been awake all night worrying about it. I don't want to see him again now. I don't *ever* want to see him again!'

'Why don't you go and speak to Sister Malcolm and ask to be moved to a different ward?' Poppy said. 'You don't have to say exactly why, just say you want a change.'

'She did say we should go to her if we had any problems,' Matthews added.

'What about his ring?'

'Give it back!' Poppy and Matthews said together.

'You don't even have to see him,' Poppy added. 'I'll do it. I'll take it to his ward and hand it to whoever's guarding the door.'

Jameson felt around the back of her neck to undo the clasp of the gold chain, slipped off the ring and gave it to Poppy. 'His name is Reinhart Teichmann.' She printed it carefully in the margin of the newspaper she held, then tore off the strip and gave it to Poppy. 'Put the ring in an envelope or something; please don't let the orderlies see what it is.' She gave a huge sniff. 'I don't want him to get into trouble.'

Matthews looked at her watch and nudged Poppy. 'The bus! We've got to go.'

Poppy stood up. 'It'll be all right, Jameson,' she said. 'Sister Malcolm will help.'

That evening, Jameson told Poppy and Matthews that she had been transferred to Hut 48, which was a medical unit dealing with those men with serious diseases picked up on the battlefield: trench fever, dysentery, influenza and so on.

'Sister Malcolm was very nice,' she said. 'I told her I was unhappy in that ward, and she said that seeing as I'd practised my nursing on German officers I should now be ready for some British boys.' She looked at Poppy anxiously. 'But did you give the ring back?'

Poppy nodded. 'It was easy. I put it in an envelope with his name on and gave it to the guard at the door.'

'And he didn't ask anything?'

'Well, he wanted to know where it had come from and I just said it was lost property – it turned up in the laundry basket.'

Jameson pressed her hand. 'Thanks. Thanks, both of you. You know, I truly never would have . . .'

'No, of course you wouldn't,' Poppy said.

YWCA Hostel,
Southampton

10th December 1915

Dear Miss Luttrell,

I am so sorry I haven't written for what seems like weeks (but is probably more like months), but I'm still here and frightfully busy. I've realised how lucky I am to be working under Sister Kay, as some VADs work for sisters who don't let them do anything remotely medical. One girl I know spends her whole working day scrubbing out lockers. When she gets to the end of the ward she starts back at the beginning again!

We have had a small scandal here at the hostel: one of the girls got rather too fond of a German prisoner of war she was looking after. He gave her a ring and seemed very keen on her – then asked too many questions about troopships. My friend Matthews and I were rather horrified and persuaded her to transfer to a different ward, which she did quite willingly. Without telling her, Matthews then wrote an anonymous letter to Matron-in-Charge saying that they should keep an eye on this particular prisoner and that he should not be allowed to form liaisons with any young VADs in future. (We didn't tell our friend about this because she's still rather soft on him.)

I must dash now! I'm sure I don't have to tell you how rushed we always are, so that half the time we have to skip meals to fit everything in. And Netley is so vast that

I reckon I walk a couple of marathons in the course of a day. We VADs are always making trips to the cobblers to get our shoes repaired!

Hoping you are very well indeed.
With love,

Poppy

At the end of that week Poppy couldn't resist counting the days since she'd written to Freddie and calculating when she might expect a reply: if he wrote by the fifteenth of December and she wrote back straight away, then there might be time for one more letter each before Christmas.

She thought about him whenever there was space in her mind. At two o'clock one morning she was shocked to discover that she couldn't decide which would be more awful: finding out that he'd been killed, or finding out that he didn't love her. Still sleepless at three, she realised that she was being entirely wicked and it didn't matter if he loved her or not – what mattered was that he should get through the war alive.

Our time will come, she thought over and over.

'Have you written to your wife to ask her for some photographs of you for the FR Unit?' Poppy asked Private Williams one morning.

He nodded, brandished his notepad and scribbled something. *Not told her what for*, it said.

'She doesn't know about your injury?' Poppy asked.

He shook his head. *Not telling her.*

'Where does she live?'

Cornwall. Too far to come.

'It is a long journey,' Poppy agreed. Not only were fares expensive, but connections were unreliable and trains mostly ran for the convenience of troops and those on war-related work. 'Maybe, by the time she arrives, you'll have your new face.'

Private Williams nodded and crinkled his eyes, which was the nearest he could get to a smile, and Poppy smiled back. It got easier.

Two afternoons later, visiting time was over and Poppy was helping Nurse Gallagher on a secondary dressings round, for some of the boys' injuries were so severe that their dressings had to be renewed two or even three times a day. Poppy was now adept at rolling bandages neatly around a leg and had the lightest of touches with complicated injuries, so she'd gradually been allowed to undertake more duties. She was pinning up the bandage on a badly wounded leg when there came a sudden, blood-curdling shriek from the top of the ward.

'No!' a woman's voice screamed. 'It's not him! It can't be!' Then there was a clatter as she fell to the floor.

Sister Kay had gone to the linen store, and the only two people out of bed at that end of the room were Greenham and Morris, two 'up patients' who were at a table cutting strips of coloured paper to make paper chains. They picked up the woman and sat her, as floppy as a rag doll, in a chair by Sister's desk. A moment afterwards, Nurse Gallagher and Poppy reached her, swiftly followed by Sister.

'What on earth happened?' Sister asked, rubbing the woman's hands.

'She came in, shrieked the place down and conked out,' said Sergeant Greenham in astonishment. 'Strangest thing I ever saw.'

'Did anyone approach her? Did anyone else see anything?' Sister asked the boys in the nearby beds.

They shook their heads – they'd been busy reading, writing home or doing crossword puzzles, and hadn't seen her come in.

Poppy then became aware that, in the bed just behind her, Private Williams was making noises in the back of his throat. Urgent, animal-like noises of distress – the only sounds he could utter. He beckoned to Poppy, his eyes showing panic, and waved his notepad, on which he'd written *Close screens. Hide.*

Poppy looked at him questioningly, trying to understand what had gone on. 'Of course,' she said, and she wheeled the curtained screens across the end of his bed so that no one could see him. 'Is there anything else?'

He scribbled on the pad again. *My wife.*

Poppy looked at him blankly, then realised what he meant and gasped. 'Oh, I'm so sorry!' She lowered her voice. 'Your wife shouldn't have been allowed to come into the ward without speaking to Sister – she likes to see families in advance to tell them if there are any . . . Because we would have . . .' But her great pity for Private Williams made her throat ache with the effort of trying not to cry, and she asked him to excuse her.

On the other side of the screens, Nurse Gallagher was holding a bottle of smelling salts under the woman's nose.

'My husband . . . My husband . . .' the woman said faintly.

'She's speaking about Private Williams,' Poppy said.

Sister nodded. 'I see.' She addressed the woman. 'I'm afraid he's been terribly badly injured, Mrs Williams. He can't talk. Someone should have informed you before you got here.'

'His face . . . awful . . . ghastly.'

'If I'd known you were coming I could have explained. Someone should have written to you. *He* should have written to you.'

'Ravaged. Destroyed!' She gave a great sob. 'He was always such a good-looking man.'

'Mrs Williams,' Sister said, 'there are things that can be done to reconstruct your husband's face, but it will take time. You will have to be patient.'

'How can I let the children see him? How can we go out anywhere? People will point at him in the street!' Mrs Williams's voice rose hysterically. 'What shall I say to people? Someone must help me!'

Sister looked at the woman keenly. 'Mrs Williams, you must remember that Private Williams is the patient in this ward, not you. Everything we do here will be to help *him*.'

The woman made a bleating noise.

'Perhaps, now you're here, you could at least have a word with him. We can cover his . . .'

'I can't!' Mrs Williams said abruptly. 'I don't want to. I don't know what to say . . . I can't bear to see him looking like that!'

'Very well, it's up to you,' Sister said. 'But I think that when you get back home you might regret not speaking to him.'

By way of an answer, the woman looked desperately at those surrounding her, then jumped up and ran for the door.

Poppy went to go after her, but Sister waved at her to sit down.

'A rather silly woman, I'm afraid,' she said in a low voice. 'But what could one possibly say?'

Poppy knew what she meant: there was no simple answer.

Chapter Twenty-Four

Dottyville

Dear Sis,
This is a funny place and no mistake. Once a day we go into a room and they shout at us and let off fireworks and make other loud noises like slaming doors and so on and they say it is to get us used to what it is like in the trenches so they can get us out there again. Of corse it is NOTHING LIKE the trenches because there is no mud and no danger and no dead bodies but i have learnd to play act and i pretend to be fritened along with the other mateys and shake and crawl under the beds to get away.

They just want to get us all back there – i know they are desperate for recruits because more and more are dying and the truth is coming through about what it is like so that men are not joining up now. Also they have cut down *the training time, so i have heard. One day you are a milkman the next you are killing people (or more likly being killed).*

But anyway for the time being my headaches have stopped and at least I am up here in Scotland and not stretched out on barbed wire being targit practise for Jerry. i will stay here as long as i can and it strikes me i ought to thank your doctor friend who must have worked a flanker so i could come here.

i have written to Ma and the girls and wonder if you will be going home for Christmas to see them. i suppose not. We make cards here, for therapy they call it, and i am sending you one with this letter.

Your brother Billy x x x

Poppy read the letter on the way to work, shaking her head over Billy's description of his treatment. As he was no longer on active service, she supposed his letters weren't checked by the censor, but even so, he'd been taking a huge risk by telling her he was only acting at being frightened. At least, though, he'd remembered to thank Michael Archer.

Her brother's Christmas postcard (a tree, coloured in carefully, as a child would do it, with a cut-out gold star on the top) gave her the idea of sending a Christmas card to Freddie. A friendly card to wish him Season's Greetings, which might possibly nudge him into sending a card back. Thinking about it now, she began to wonder if she *had* been too frank, too truthful about her feelings. Boys were different — everyone knew that. If a girl was too keen it scared them off. On the other hand, what was the point of having a relationship with someone if you couldn't tell them your true feelings?

Christmas cards from anxious relatives had already begun appearing on the boys' lockers. They tended to be sentimental affairs: angels hovering over soldiers' heads, soldiers asleep and dreaming of their loved ones, or cosy firesides with pleas to keep the home fires burning. Searching in the shops, none seemed suitable for the sort of relationship she had with Freddie. Finally, on her afternoon off, Poppy found a card with a picture of a girl decorating a Christmas tree and these words below:

> *It's only a simple little card,*
> *But it comes from me to say,*
> *I was thinking of you when I posted it.*
> *Are you thinking of me today?*

This, she thought, was exactly right, and she just added her name and a line of kisses. As she posted it she couldn't help hoping that it would get redirected from his unit to his home, and that his mother might see it . . .

*

A few mornings later, Poppy managed to catch Michael Archer on his way out of the ward. To the amusement of both of them, the boys in the nearby beds suddenly stopped perusing the newspapers and began singing, *If I had someone at home like you,* almost as if they'd rehearsed it. As well as making Poppy laugh, it also had the effect of making her blush, which seemed to please them even more.

'Nice to see you in the pink!' called Private Mackay.

She tried to ignore them. 'May I speak to you a moment, Doctor Archer?'

'Of course, Pearson. And please do call me Michael.'

'I couldn't possibly! Sister would explode.'

'Would she really?' he said with interest. 'Of course, I don't suppose that *you* have a first name.'

Poppy hid a smile. 'I have, but I'm not allowed to say what it is.'

'*I would fall in love every day . . .*' came from the boys.

Poppy turned to glare at them, trying to look fierce. 'I do apologise,' she said to Michael Archer. 'They're not being very respectful.' She lowered her voice so that their conversation couldn't be overheard. 'I just wanted to let you know that my brother is doing quite well in Scotland. He asked me to thank you for helping him.'

'That's good,' Michael Archer said, nodding. 'What do you think he'll do when his time there is up?'

'I've no idea,' Poppy said. This question had been worrying her. 'I'm afraid Billy's just not what you might call patriotic – or even loyal.' She lowered her voice to a whisper. 'That's wrong, isn't it? Everyone should want to fight for their country – for the glory of the motherland, as they say.'

Michael Archer glanced around the ward, at the beds containing forty or so arm-less or leg-less men. 'Sometimes glory is in short supply, Pearson. Sometimes I wonder if people like your brother *have* got it right. If everyone refused to fight . . .'

Poppy looked at him, wide-eyed. 'But you can't mean that or you wouldn't be doing what you are doing.'

'I'm not fighting, I'm just picking up the pieces,' Michael Archer said. 'As you are. We're both doing the same job.'

The boys finished that particular song and there was a moment's silence. To fill the gap in the conversation, Poppy asked, 'Will you be at the hospital over Christmas?'

'Indeed I will,' he said. 'I've already applied to carve Hut 59's Christmas goose.'

'Really?' Poppy asked, laughing

He nodded. 'Each hut gets one doctor or surgeon assigned to them on Christmas Day.'

'I'm on Christmas duty, too,' Poppy said. 'Sister's asked me to collect gifts for the boys' Christmas stockings.'

'So you're kind of like the Christmas fairy?'

'Kind of.' Poppy laughed. 'I've asked one of the comforts groups in Southampton to knit fifty loose-loop stockings, each with a tie that will knot over the end of a hospital bed, and I'm collecting gifts to go in them.' She hesitated. 'Would it be rude to ask if you've qualified yet?'

'It wouldn't be rude at all. I have indeed!' he said.

'So, will you be staying here at Netley?'

'Only until my placement comes through. I'll be sent to Flanders then, but I don't know quite where.'

'In the thick of the fighting?'

He nodded. 'Probably a field hospital – as near to the front line as possible. It's been established that the sooner injured men can get medical help, the more likely it is that their lives can be saved.' He looked at her keenly. 'You know, they're going to need a lot more VADs out there soon. There's going to be a big push in the spring.'

'I know, but . . .' Poppy's voice trailed away. She and Matthews had talked about getting closer to the action, working nearer the front line, but the thought of such a move was too heart-stoppingly frightening, too arduous, too terrifying. Also, staying safe in Southampton meant she'd see Freddie every time he came through on leave.

'Not that you're not doing sterling work here,' Michael Archer said, with his wide smile. 'And I'm sure that your boys here wouldn't thank me for encouraging you to leave them.'

Poppy was going to reply, but Sister Kay called out, '*Pearson!*' and she had to excuse herself and dash off. She did so accompanied by a rousing rendition of *You Planted a Rose in the Garden of Love.*

*

Two days before Christmas, when Poppy had almost given up hope of hearing from him, a postcard arrived from Freddie, enclosed in an envelope. The picture showed an infantryman, a sailor, an airman and a VAD standing under a Union Jack, with a banner saying, *England knows that every man will do his duty.* On the back, in very large writing, it said, *Fondest love, Freddie.*

Poppy showed it to Matthews, who thought it was a bit off. 'There's a VAD in the scene so it should say every man and *woman!*' Turning it over, she read the back. 'That's nice, though. *Fondest love . . .*'

'But in such large handwriting!' Poppy said. 'As if he couldn't think of anything else to say and needed to fill up the space.'

'And there's nothing about you meeting up when he comes through Southampton.'

'Oh, well, he probably doesn't know exactly when he's coming back,' Poppy said. 'After all . . .' She looked at Matthews.

'. . . there's a war on,' they chorused.

Our time will come, Poppy thought to herself. But, it seemed, not just yet.

Christmas Eve dawned fine, bright and frosty, both the sky and sea a cornflower blue. Going into the hospital that morning, Poppy hoped she'd find the boys full of Christmas spirit and perhaps even hopeful about the war going the Allies' way in the coming year. She was to be disappointed, however, because most of them had lost any earlier optimism along with their limbs. Many, also, had friends or family members who'd not survived to reach this second Christmas of the war. For them, the other depressing thing was that warnings had been sent from the top generals to the boys at the front to say that there must be no consorting with the enemy this year, no communal singing of *Silent Night* or England versus Germany games of football. This command had not gone down well and it was whispered that morale among the troops was low.

At four o'clock that afternoon, the ward became a little more cheerful when Poppy went around hanging Christmas stockings on the boys' bed rails, then put up homemade paper chains as well as red, white and blue bunting which had been donated by a Good Egg.

It had been announced that, this Christmas, Princess Mary would not be sending out the little brass boxes containing small gifts that every soldier had received the year before. There were so many troops out there now, in such far-flung corners of Europe, that it was thought the delivery of such boxes would be impracticable. Poppy was disappointed about this, but had accumulated a good assortment of gifts for the boys' Christmas stockings: notebooks, pencils and sharpeners, chocolate bars, soap, packets of cigarettes and special boxes of matches bearing Christmas pictures. She had also obtained some little metal toy cars and vans on the assumption that all men were boys at heart.

The cheery feeling disappeared immediately, however, when news came from Private Taylor's ward that he had died in his sleep.

His ward sister came in to tell Sister Kay and her team the news. 'He rallied a little when his mother came to stay nearby,' she said, 'but I don't think he ever really meant to live. When she went back home a couple of days ago, it freed him to slip away.'

'He told me that he was dreading the idea of Christmas without his brother,' Sister Kay said with a sigh.

When the other ward sister had left, Sister Kay said, 'While we're all together, I've something to tell you.'

Nurse Gallagher, Moffat and Poppy looked at her expectantly.

'I'm afraid this will be my last month at Netley,' she went on. 'In the New Year you'll be working under another sister. A new sister will mean new rules, of course, but I have the greatest confidence in all of you.'

There was a moment's shocked silence, during which Poppy felt she wanted to hug the gaunt figure and ask her not to leave. 'That's really sad news,' she said.

'We'll miss you dreadfully,' added Nurse Gallagher.

'Are you retiring?' Poppy asked.

Sister looked taken aback. 'Hardly. How old do you think I am? There's a few years' life in me yet!'

'Of course!' Poppy said, blushing. 'I didn't mean . . .'

'No, I'm going to France to run a casualty clearing station near the front line. I shall miss you all, but I can be of more use out there. I think 1916 is going to be particularly difficult.'

Poppy went back to the hostel at the normal time, ate a quick supper and then returned to Netley to fill the boys' stockings under cover of darkness. The night staff were on duty by then, the ward was quiet apart from some snoring and snuffling, and everyone was praying that no unexpected convoys of wounded would come in. Poppy did her stocking duty, then remembered that Jameson had given her a satchel containing some illustrated newspapers and magazines. Her friend, already quite settled in her new ward, had been collecting these as Christmas treats for her boys and had found herself with more than she needed. Poppy spread them out on one of the tables, then went home and, looking forward to Christmas Day, slept soundly.

The boys had all investigated the contents of their Christmas stockings by the time Poppy got to the hospital the next morning – in fact, they had already started swapping their tin cars. Breakfast went much as usual, except there was cream and brown sugar for the porridge as a special treat, and afterwards someone put on a recording of Christmas carols and everyone joined in the singing. Following this came a game of bed-to-bed softball and some magic tricks from Sergeant Carter, whilst, in the background, the ordinary life of the ward went on: bandages were changed, lesions cleansed, drugs given out, open wounds packed and bed sores treated.

The roast goose or turkey – one for each ward – came courtesy of the local farmers, and it seemed to be no surprise to the boys that Doctor Michael Archer, wearing a red Santa Claus hat, turned up to carve theirs. Around this time a bunch of mistletoe also appeared, hanging in the doorway tied up with medical tape, and this sight caused Poppy to receive a look of warning from Sister Kay. Knowing exactly what she meant – and much to the boys' disappointment – Poppy made sure that she didn't walk directly underneath it while Michael Archer was around.

At about two o'clock, after the young doctor had gone, those boys who didn't want an afternoon nap put on their dressing gowns and gathered around one of the tables, reading out snippets from the Christmas magazines to each other. Poppy listened to them idly. The King and Queen were going to be at Sandringham for the festivities; the famous pianist Miss Marie Novello was in London for a performance at the Coliseum; Miss Ellaline Terriss was appearing in *Bluebell in Fairyland* at the Prince's Theatre.

'Have you seen this photograph of Ellaline Terriss, nurse!' Sergeant Carter said to Poppy. 'You look just like her.'

'I'm sure I don't!' Poppy held out her hand for the centre pages of the paper. 'May I see?'

Moffat peered at the page as it was being handed across. 'No! Miss Terriss is at least ten years older than Pearson!'

'Well, I reckon she's your double,' said Sergeant Carter. 'Either that or you've got a part-time job up in London o' nights.'

Poppy smoothed out the paper and studied the picture. She was flattered to be thought to look like the glamorous actress, but Moffat was right – Miss Terriss was at least ten years older. She was just about to hand the newspaper back when her eye was caught by a small, square photograph, one of five in a column down the side of the page. The headline was *Christmas Romances* and the photographs were all of young ladies who had recently become engaged to be married. And one of them looked very much like . . .

Poppy gave a cry of shock and, in her haste to see the photograph close up, practically snatched the magazine back from Sergeant Carter.

'So sorry!' she cried to the astonished men. 'Will you all please excuse me a moment.' Jumping up, she ran into the kitchen.

Yes, it *was* her. The same glossy bob, the same perfect smile. Miss Philippa Cardew.

Underneath the photograph it said:

Cardew and de Vere
The engagement is announced between Miss Philippa Imogen Cardew and Second Lt Frederick James de Vere. The bridegroom is at present on active service and, following his return to this country on leave, the wedding will take place quietly on New Year's Day.

Chapter Twenty-Five

I t was all over. The grand love affair that Poppy had envisaged was finished before it had properly started.

At first she didn't believe it. Surely it was some sort of joke? Or it was a mistake, a foolish mix-up at the magazine offices. But then again it *must* be true, because there it was, printed in black and white, with a photograph and names and everything. It *was* true, and Freddie didn't love her – had never loved her. He'd just been toying with her affections, leading her on, pretending, lying, acting out a part.

Furious, her heart pounding, different scenarios for revenge came into Poppy's head. She'd find out where the wedding was to be held and go along – when the rector asked in church if there was any impediment to the marriage, she'd stand up. She'd contact his mother and say that they'd had a relationship. She'd write to Freddie's commanding officer and say that he hadn't behaved in a manner that befitted an officer and a gentle-man. She'd tell not only Miss Cardew, but the whole village, so that everyone would know how beastly he'd been.

But she didn't do any of these things.

Instead she thought about it while she was serving tea and Christmas cake, then quietly spoke to Sister Kay and took her notepaper and pen.

YWCA Hostel,
Southampton

25th December 1915

The Recruitment Office,
Devonshire House,
London,
SW1

Dear Madam,
I am a nursing VAD presently working at Netley Hut Hospital. I am hardworking and diligent, and believe I could serve my country better if I was working as a VAD in France or Belgium. I am therefore applying for a posi-tion at either a field hospital or a casualty clearing station as close to the front line as possible.

I am not quite of the minimum age for what I know to be dangerous work, but in view of my experience and taking into consideration the great demand for nurses, I hope you are prepared to overlook this. My present nursing sister, Sister Kay, has kindly said she will back my application and supervise my progress.

I look forward to hearing from you at your earliest convenience.

Yours faithfully,

Miss Poppy Pearson

Some Notes from the Author

I don't remember learning about the war at school, so researching it from the point of view of one of the young volunteer nurses who served during it has been both eye-opening and humbling. More than 70,000 VADs (Voluntary Aid Detachment) were recruited to serve as nurses, ambulance drivers, cooks and stretcher bearers during the Great War. Two thirds of VADs were women or girls.

As soon as I knew I was writing this book, I went to the Imperial War Museum in London, which holds a huge amount of wartime memorabilia. Unfortunately, when I got there I discovered that, just three days before my visit, the World War I section had been closed temporarily in order to set up new displays in readiness for 2014, the centenary of the outbreak of the war. It will be open again by the time this book is published and should be the first port of call to anyone who wants to find out more.

I found other places to do my research, including the British Red Cross Museum in London, where the staff were most helpful, and the amazing new interactive museum in Ypres, Belgium, which was a fiercely contested city throughout the war. There are a great many museums in this area, including small, family-run bases situated on what was actually the front line, with shored-up trenches still in place. Visiting one of these museums on a dark November day in the pouring rain, standing beside a lone piper in full Highland dress playing a lament, was a memorable moment. It also made me decide that I would like to write a second book where Poppy goes to work as a nurse in Flanders, very close to the front line.

As well as the books listed in the *Bibliography* I made use of the many internet sites devoted to different aspects of the war, especially the excellent *The Long, Long Trail* at *www.1914-1918.net*, and the marvellous *Scarletfinders* at *www.scarletfinders.co.uk*, which is specifically about British military nurses and has a huge and fascinating section about VADs plus lots of photographs.

Much has been written about the bravery and humour of the ordinary soldier, the Tommy. Photographs of Tommies going off to fight, waving their tin hats and cheering, are especially heartbreaking when you learn that whole platoons of young men were killed or injured in one battle, many only seventeen or eighteen years of age.

Some soldiers, like Billy, couldn't cope with the carnage they were confronted with. They either ran away, inflicted wounds on themselves, went mad with terror or simply refused to fight. Most of these men were court-martialled and faced an instant death by firing squad. Some 306 soldiers died in this way. Relatives of these men have been active in trying to obtain a pardon for them and to have their names put on war memorials, arguing that they weren't criminals, but were suffering severe mental trauma.

Conditions in field hospitals – that is, those close to the front line ('in the field') – were poor and there were no antibiotics at this time. Although the importance of hygiene was understood, it was difficult to keep things sterile when men came into the operating theatre badly injured, gashed all over by rusty barbed wire or covered in caked-on mud. Those with major injuries had very little chance of survival. If wounds were very extensive, they were often packed with dried sphagnum moss. This was highly absorbent and could hold quantities of liquid and blood, like a natural type of cotton wool. If they were lucky, those with facial wounds were treated at one of the facial reconstruction units, known by Tommies as the 'tin noses shops', within a hospital. The most famous of these, Queen Mary's Hospital in Sidcup, Kent, provided pioneering plastic surgery to those with injuries to their faces. The skill of the surgeons was remarkable and the patients were treated with care and compassion. However, although some patients endured years of operations in the hopes of making themselves look even passable, many still struggled to re-enter society. The extreme psychological trauma of having bad facial injuries must have been very great indeed.

This is a work of fiction and, although I have researched the period and read diaries and first-hand accounts of the war, all the characters are fictitious. Some of the places are not, however: Netley Hut Hospital is very much based on the real hospital of the same name in Southampton which was demolished in 1966. The war poet Wilfred Owen was briefly treated at Netley in 1917 before being transferred to 'Dottyville', as the patients called Craiglockhart War Hospital in Edinburgh. Although I would have liked Owen to have a walk-on part in this story, he was there in 1917 and *Poppy* is set in 1915.

Airey House is fictional but is typical of the many great houses up and down the country which became hospitals or convalescent homes for war casualties. Some of these were official and came under the auspices of the War Office; others were run by wealthy women who wanted to do something concrete to help the war effort. When the war ended some of these great houses were never reclaimed by their owners, often because they could no longer get the staff to run them. Many former male servants – grooms, valets, butlers and so on – had become casualties of the war, while many female servants had found more varied professions. This era was a time of great social change and the women who had taken on men's jobs, and proved themselves more than capable of doing so, didn't want to stay below stairs. It took until 1928 for all women to get the vote, but they were well on their way.

If you enjoyed *Poppy*, look out for the sequel, *Poppy in the Field*, publishing in May 2015.

Bibliography

Appleton, Edith, *A Nurse at the Front: The First World War Diaries of Sister Edith Appleton*, Simon and Schuster, 2012

Atkinson, Diane, *Elsie and Mairi Go to War: Two Extraordinary Women on the Western Front*, Arrow, 2010

Bagnold, Enid, *A Diary Without Dates*, Virago, 1978

Bowser, Thekla, *Britain's Civilian Volunteers: Authorised Story of British Voluntary Aid Detachment Work*, Forgotten Books, 2012

Brittain, Vera, *Testament of Youth*, Virago, 1978

Doyle, Peter, *First World War Britain*, Shire Publications, 2012

MacDonald, Lyn, *The Roses of No Man's Land*, Penguin, 1993

Rathbone, Irene, *We That Were Young*, Virago, 1988

Tapert, Annette, *Despatches from the Heart: An Anthology of Letters from the Front*, Hamish Hamilton, 1984

Van der Kloot, William, *World War One Fact Book*, Amberley Publishing, 2011

Poppy's story continues in the sequel,

Poppy in the Field,

publishing May 2015.